To Julie

# Dispense With Death

### A novel by

### Peter Mulholland

Copyright © 2013 by Peter Mulholland

ISBN-13: 978-1490904177

ISBN-10: 1490904174

All rights reserved including the rights to reproduce this book or portions thereof in any form whatsoever.

## Disclaimer

This is a work of fiction. Names, characters, businesses, places, events and incidents are either the products of the author's imagination or used in a fictitious manner. Any resemblance to actual persons, living or dead, or actual events is purely coincidental.

Cover photograph: Peter Mulholland

Chapter 1 .................................................... 4
Chapter 2 .................................................... 5
Chapter 3 .................................................. 10
Chapter 4 .................................................. 16
Chapter 5 .................................................. 29
Chapter 6 .................................................. 31
Chapter 7 .................................................. 38
Chapter 8 .................................................. 41
Chapter 9 .................................................. 59
Chapter 10 ................................................ 65
Chapter 11 ................................................ 77
Chapter 12 ................................................ 89
Chapter 13 ................................................ 96
Chapter 14 .............................................. 103
Chapter 15 .............................................. 114
Chapter 16 .............................................. 122
Chapter 17 .............................................. 131
Chapter 18 .............................................. 145
Chapter 19 .............................................. 151
Chapter 20 .............................................. 158
Chapter 21 .............................................. 164
About the author ..................................... 166

## Chapter 1

The boy was only eighteen. He had been rushed to hospital accident and emergency department at 5.47pm. The rear seat passenger in a car driven by his friend, he had been catapulted between the front seats and through the windscreen when the car skidded and crashed down the motorway embankment.

The medical and nursing staff did not hold out much hope when he was admitted, but they did their best. At 7.03pm it was over - the boy was dead.

The old woman had lived alone since her husband died six years previously. She was seventy-six years old and could not get out very often. She had a history of heart trouble, not helped by her inability to take her prescribed medicine regularly.

The home help arrived for her regular Tuesday visit. She was not surprised when there was no answer to her knock at the door - a gradual loss of hearing over the past year was but one of Mrs Greenford's many problems. Using the key that she had been given she let herself into the flat. Mrs Greenford was still in bed. Thinking that she was sleeping the home help tried to rouse the old woman - without success.

The doctor arrived twenty minutes later. When he saw Mrs Greenford he knew straight away - it was probably an unexpected benefit - that she had passed away in her sleep. He started to write out the death certificate.

**Chapter 2**

7.30pm and his shift was coming to an end. It was a day that Tom Donaldson thought that he would never see again - the day when he would once again put in an eight hour shift to earn a wage. Four years earlier he had had a good job working in the local car plant. Twenty-nine years he had worked there. It was the only job he had known, joining straight from school. But the end had been in sight - Tom had seen that. The company's model range was hopelessly outdated and there had not been any investment in new equipment for years.

It was on his forty fourth birthday that the news that he had been expecting came. The plant was to shut in three months time, at the end of October. With his years of long service Tom knew that he would get a good redundancy payment, but how long would that last if he could not get another job. Unemployment in the area was already high. The closure of the car plant would make it much worse. At his age he would be lucky to get another job.

On the scrapheap at 44.

The first two months had been all right. It was just like an extended holiday and meant that Tom could spend more time on preparations for the Christmas season than he had been able to in previous years. However, once the New Year festivities were over he had realised that he had nothing to look forward to. Endless days spent walking in the local parks, watching television or just staring at four walls.

He had lost count of the number of jobs that he had applied for - in three and a half years it must have been well over two hundred. Always the same reply - if there was a reply at all. He had resigned himself to never working again when he had heard about this job. Previously Tom had thought of a hospital as somewhere to be avoided - only to be entered if strictly necessary. But the offer of a job could not be passed up, when he had been convinced that he should apply.

Most of his first day had been spent finding his way around the sprawling mass of the hospital. It was a mixture of old and new and was one of the largest hospitals in the country with over two thousand beds covering every age range from neonate to geriatric, and virtually every medical speciality.

To start with he was to work in the "pool"- a group of about thirty porters that worked in three shifts and carried out general duties in the medical, surgical and geriatric wards. His duties would involve taking samples to the laboratories, such as biochemistry and haematology, and helping to transfer patients from ward to ward and from ward to theatre. The heavy aspect of the work did not bother him. He had never shirked hard work before and he did not intend to start now. And anyway, it was better than sitting at home all day.

"Right Tom, one more job to do before you finish."

It was the voice of young Eric Nash, one of the other pool porters. Tom had been working with him all day to learn the ropes.

"Bring the trolley."

This was one of the jobs that Tom was not looking forward to. The trolley was like a metal coffin on wheels, which was an apt description as it was used to transport patients who had died, either in a ward or in theatre to the mortuary.

"Where are we taking it?"

"Theatre 3. Car crash victim. Young lad of eighteen."

Just eighteen, the same age as his own daughter, Becky. She would be about halfway through her shift now, working with the psychogeriatric patients, here in the same hospital. Becky was the one who had suggested that he apply for the job when she heard of the vacancy. Ever since Tom had bought her a nurse outfit for her ninth birthday nursing was all that she had wanted to do with her life. She was now in her second year of training and was enjoying virtually every minute of it.

Now they were heading up the cold, damp corridor that leads to the mortuary, having collected the body from the theatre. The corridor filled one with a sense of gloom and depression before one even reached the mortuary.

The room was just how Tom imagined it would be, although he had thought that somehow it would be different from the way that it was portrayed on television. But, there, in the middle of the floor, were two large tables, surrounded by a clean, tiled floor with channels set into it for ease of cleaning.

From behind the door appeared the mortuary attendant. Tom jumped at his sudden, silent, appearance.

"This the stiff? Sling him up there, will you."

Dispense With Death

Tom was taken aback at the man's disregard for the corpse and was about to protest, but the look Eric gave him, told him to keep quiet. They transferred the corpse onto the nearest of the two tables and pushed the trolley back out through the double swing doors. As they headed back down the corridor Tom turned to Eric.

"Why did you make me keep quiet? What a disgrace the way he treated that poor boy's body. Doesn't he have any respect for the dead?"

"Don't go losing the rag" replied Eric calmly "How would you like to work in there eight hours a day, without a living soul to talk to? Just be grateful that he didn't know that it was your first time in the mortuary. He can have a wicked sense of humour. A couple of years back he knew that there was a new porter bringing up a body. He lay on the table and covered most of his body with a drape. Have you met Toni Niglarti yet?"

"Yes."

"Well, he was with this rookie porter, and he and Ron back there had planned this as a sort of initiation into the job. Toni and the young porter went up to the mortuary. Must have been about 10 o'clock at night and the place was in darkness except for a couple of sidelights. Suddenly this 'dead' body rose from the table. You've never seen anyone move so fast as that porter did. Toni eventually caught up with him back at the 'pool'. He was ready to leave there and then, but he eventually calmed down."

"And what happened to him?"

"You're talking to him."

**Chapter 3**

The bell always seemed to ring when he was on the 'phone. And there would be no-one else in the department to answer it.

"I'll be with you in a minute" shouted Ben Brosan.

He put down the 'phone and walked out to the hatch where the nurses handed in indents and prescriptions to the pharmacy. There was a nurse waiting there. It was her blond hair that he noticed first, then he saw her eyes. She had the bluest eyes that he had ever seen. Ben dragged his mind back to work and took the indent from her. A couple of minutes work and he was back to give her her order. Becky Donaldson. He saw her name as she signed for the drugs. A strange feeling came over Ben as she walked out the door. No, it couldn't be. You only read about it in soppy novels. Love at first sight? He did not believe it, but how else could he explain the feeling inside him. Ben knew that somehow he had to see her again.

All throughout the afternoon Ben could not get the nurse out of his mind. As he drove home he was still thinking about her when a sharp blast on a car horn brought him back to reality. His car was halfway onto a roundabout. He may have been in a romantic mood, but the driver of the battered old Nissan, six inches from his door mirror, was not whispering sweet nothings in Ben's ear. Ben smiled sheepishly, waved in apology, and drove off as fast as he could. This only served to irritate the other driver even more and Ben could hear the diminishing sound of the car horn as he sped down the road. Ten minutes later, and he was back at the flat.

The only problem with living in a flat was that there never seemed to be enough parking spaces for everyone. Today was no exception and Ben eventually found a space for the Triumph about 150 yards from his entrance. He was just glad that it was not raining. It had been a busy day and he was tired. Slowly he trudged up the three flights of stairs to his top floor flat. The flat had been purchased when he had a full time job. Some money left to him by his grandfather had covered the deposit and his grandfather's furniture had furnished the flat.

It had taken two long, painful years from the diagnosis of cancer until his grandfather's death. Ben wished that he had been taken quickly and quietly, like his grandmother. It was heartrending to watch the gradual decline in the proud old man.

The previous owner of the flat had obviously decorated the flat in the early Seventies and had never touched it since. Purple wallpaper in the lounge toned tastefully with the orange carpet on the floor. Around the edges of the carpet the floorboards were visible - stained a delicate shade of black. The carpet had gone straight away replaced by a neutral coloured fitted one. The wallpaper was stripped and replaced with a delicately patterned blown vinyl. Both bedrooms and the bathroom had followed a similar style to the lounge, and a similar fate befell each.

His grandfather's furniture, although not modern, fitted in well with Ben's living style and gave the flat a lived-in look. So much nicer than some of the studio flats that he had looked at when he first started flat hunting.

As he reheated the leftover chilli from the previous day Ben reflected on the afternoon. Even the near miss in the car could not take his mind off Becky. He had never before felt the way that he did now, but then he had never had much experience with girls. Throughout school he had never seemed to have the time to go out with girls. His studies seemed to take up all of his time. Of course he flirted with the girls in the class and they seemed to like him, but it never went any farther. It was the same at university. There were always parties, but apart from a couple of short lived romances he had not had a proper long term girlfriend for years. At the first opportunity he would ask her for a date. But how to go about it? The chat-up lines that he had used at school would serve him no use now. He would just have to wait and see if and when the opportunity arose. One thing was for certain, to try and ask her while she was standing at the hatch would be potentially too embarrassing.

He switched on the television and sat down to eat his dinner. After that he would spend the rest of the night watching TV, if there was something decent on, which was unlikely these days. Everyone seemed to complain about how bad TV was these days. It was probably the same thing that had people longing for the 'good old days'. Memory blocked out the bad and only retained the good times. A glance at the TV guide showed that the only things worth watching were an old John Wayne film at 9 o'clock and the golf highlights around midnight. Clearing up his dishes Ben settled down on the sofa with the book that he had been reading.

\*\*\*

It was to be three days before Ben saw Becky again. In that time he had managed to keep his mind on work but, to his surprise, he still felt the same way. The ward sister from Becky's ward had 'phoned over to have some drugs returned to the pharmacy. Ben had taken the call and volunteered to go over. When he was in the ward he had managed to strike up a conversation with Becky and asked her out. To his surprise she had agreed. They set a date for that evening.

Ben drew up outside Becky's house. The top was down on the car to take advantage of one of the rare summer evenings.

"Hi" called Becky as she ran down the garden path. "Nice car."

"It's all right in this weather. In the winter, when the rain drips in, it's not so nice. You don't mind the hood being down, do you?"

"No. I've never been in a sports car before. It'll be a new experience. Where are we going?"

"How about a drive down to the coast? It's too nice an evening to sit in a cinema or a pub. We could find somewhere with tables outside and have a drink there."

"Sounds great."

Becky had always stayed in the town. She only lived ten minutes walk from the hospital, and had played in its grounds as a little girl. After a fifth year at secondary school she had started training to be a nurse and was now nearing the end of her second year's training. Ben worked out that she would be about eighteen, maybe nineteen, years old. He was twenty four. Still, what was five or six years. They seemed to get along quite well. He pulled the car into a parking space outside a beachfront cafe and they got out. As they walked along the promenade Ben tentatively took a hold of Becky's hand and he was pleased, and relieved, to find that it wasn't drawn away.

They walked back to the cafe and sat down to have a drink. The rest of the evening was spent chatting, each relaxed in the other's company until, too soon, it was time to head for home. Ben started the car and headed out the country road that would take them back to town. After about five minutes there was a loud bang from the front of the car. Ben struggled to keep control and eventually managed to bring the car to a halt, just keeping it on the road. Jumping out he spotted the cause of the bang.

"The tyre's bust. I hope there's air in the spare. I always forget to check it when I check the others."

Becky clambered out of the car and stood at the roadside, looking at the tattered remains of the tyre.

"Well it beats running out of petrol as an excuse for stopping on a deserted country road."

Ben tried to reply but his embarrassment made it difficult.

"I'm only teasing. Judging by the state of that tyre you did well to stop the car in one piece. Let me give you a hand to get the wheel off and put on the spare. And don't say no, I'm used to working around cars. My dad worked with them for years and is always tinkering with them in his spare time."

Before he could say anything she was down helping to remove the stricken wheel. In no time at all they had the spare wheel, which thankfully had air in the tyre, bolted in place and they were on their way. The rest of the journey passed without further incident. Ben drew up outside Becky's house. He reached over and gave her a quick kiss on the cheek.

"See you tomorrow ?"

"Yes, and come here" Becky threw her arms around him and kissed him full on the lips. Ben withdrew, breathless, and before he could recover she was away. He drove back to the flat and managed to find a space just outside the front door. As he stepped out of the car a stray dog snapped at his heel. A quick stamp of the foot and a growl soon had the dog scurrying away. He ran into the close and took the stairs two at a time. He was actually looking forward to work the next day. After all he might see Becky at the hospital.

**Chapter 4**

It was 2 a.m. and 'Pip' Barton, senior house officer, was crawling into bed. He had been on duty, or on-call, for the past forty two hours. Being woken up at 1.30 a.m. just to prescribe an enema for a patient was not his idea of fun. But, there was nothing that he could do about ridiculous calls. If he complained to the consultant he would get nowhere - "Stand you in good stead for the future."

As for the ward sister, she had been there 22 years and no young doctor, or consultant for that matter, was going to tell her how to run her ward. Thank God he had only another four weeks and then it was on to obstetrics. Surely he would have an easier time of it then.

Beep. Beep. Beep. Beep.

Pip slowly opened his eyes and looked at the green display on his bedside clock. 2.37. He had been asleep for just over half an hour. If this was another enema required then it wouldn't be the patient who was getting it, and he would administer it personally. He rang the ward and heard the now familiar sound of the ward's night sister on the other end of the line.

"Ward 27. Sister Applewood speaking."

"It's Dr. Barton here. You were looking for me. Again."

"Yes, doctor. It's Mrs Shaw. She's stopped breathing and we can't get her resuscitated. We've tried everything that we can."

Pip was now wide awake and was no longer listening to the sister. The phone was dangling by the side of the bed and he was on his way out the door.

The ward was not in its usual overnight state of calm when he arrived. The screens were drawn around Mrs Shaw's bed to cordon it off from the rest of the ward. Many of the patients had been awakened by the commotion and were anxious to know what was going on. An enrolled nurse was trying to get them back to sleep. A student nurse sat shocked in the duty room. Probably her first experience of something like this thought Pip as he rushed past and stepped behind the screens.

He knew straight away that she was dead. No amount of effort on his part would bring the woman round, but he felt that he had to try. After a few minutes he gave up. As he walked back to his room Pip realised that, as the duty physician, he would have to report on the case in the morning - even though he should be off duty.

* * *

Pip was looking through Mrs Shaw's case notes when the door of the duty room opened. "Morning everyone" announced the tweed suited gentleman as he entered the room. Were it not for the stethoscope hanging out of his pocket it would have been difficult to tell that this was a doctor, let alone an eminent gastroenterologist. Dr John Strone was regarded as slightly eccentric, but an expert in his field. tweeds were his characteristic form of dress and he only wore a white coat when it was strictly necessary.

"Now Pip, tell me about this patient who died."

Dispense With Death

Pip still had Mrs Shaw's case notes in front of him, but he knew what he had to say without referring to them. "Penelope Shaw. Aged 45. Partial gastrectomy two days ago. Temperature spiked twelve hours later and started on intravenous antibiotics. Progress thereafter uneventful and a full recovery looked likely, until early this morning. Sister?"

"At 2.27 this morning" continued Sister Applewood "an enrolled nurse was checking Mrs Shaw's i/v line and noticed that she wasn't breathing. resuscitation was unsuccessful and the house officer was called."

"The patient was dead when I arrived."

"What happened prior to her breathing stopping ?"

"A new bag of antibiotic had just been connected up to her drip."

"It couldn't have been a severe reaction to the drug ?"

"Unlikely, this was her sixth dose. Normally any reaction would have shown up before now. I ordered a post mortem and the result was shown as being due to asphyxia."

"You got them to perform a post mortem at what, three in the morning ?"

"Yes."

"I bet you were popular. Go on."

"What it also shows is a high serum level of the neuro-muscular blocking agent used in her operation."

Dispense With Death

"48 hours after the operation ?"

"Yes. I've never heard of its effects re-occurring so long after an operation."

John Strone was silent. No-one spoke - it was evident that he was thinking things over and it would be a brave and foolish person who tried to derail his train of thought. Finally he broke the silence.

"We have to report this of course. It's the first time that I've ever come across this. The poor woman. She must have been in agony, even though it could only have been for a few minutes. Did no-one hear her ?"

"No doctor"

"No-one would have" said Pip "the drug would have paralysed her muscles."

"Oh yes. Quite. Get me a full report for this afternoon, would you Dr Barton ?"

Pip groaned. What he wanted to do was to get some much needed sleep, not write a report, the final version of which would not even bear his name.


Saturday. Two days later and Pip was back on duty. He had written the report as quickly as he could and then went to bed. He had a nagging doubt about Mrs Shaw's death, but what it was eluded him. He felt that he was somehow at fault, even partly, but no matter how many times he went over it in his mind he couldn't find an answer. She had died not long after one of her bags of antibiotic had been connected up but he didn't see how that could have been at fault. He had prepared the days supply all at the same time, as he always did. All the vials of drug had come from the same box. It was the third bag of the day so there couldn't have been anything wrong with them. Perhaps she was just one of those unpredictable cases that no-one could have foreseen.

He tried to put the case out of his mind and carry on with his duties. Today he was carrying the cardiac arrest page and he was certain that he was going to be busy. He decided to try and read the paper while it was still quiet and turned to the sports pages, as always the first part that he would read. How he enjoyed playing a game of football on a Saturday or going to see his local team play. At school and throughout university he had always had his Saturdays free. Since he started working in the hospital all that had changed. Now he often had to work Sunday as well as Saturday. Playing football regularly was out of the question. When he had last been at a football match he couldn't remember. Six months ? Nine months ? Even a Saturday off would be nice. This was his fourth Saturday on in a row. At least if it was busy it wouldn't be too bad in that the time would pass quickly. Then again maybe today all that he would have to do would be to read the papers and drink interminable mugs of coffee.

Just at that the bleep went off. It took a moment to register that it was the cardiac arrest bleep. "Here we go" he thought "I spoke too soon."

There were trays of drugs ready prepared for such emergencies on the wards, each containing all the necessary drugs for immediate treatment. Pip found what he was looking for, drew the contents of the vial into a syringe and injected it into the man. He waited.

Something was wrong - there was no response. He tried again - still nothing. Now he was onto the drugs on a second tray and still nothing was happening apart from the man's life ebbing away. The monotone of the ECG monitor droned mournfully on. Only one more thing to try - he picked up the paddle of the defibrillator machine. "Stand clear".

A powerful bolt of electricity shot through the man's body. Nothing. he tried again. Still no response. There was no more he could do and reluctantly Pip gave up the struggle. He sat down, drained by his efforts. Why was there no response to the drugs - he would have expected some. Before he had a chance to gather his thoughts the bleep played its tune again. Another arrest - this time in the ward next door. Pip rushed in and started the same procedure that he had just carried out a few minutes beforehand. He couldn't believe it - he was getting no response this time either. In desperation he shouted to a nurse to open the drug cupboard and get him injections from there rather than using yet another cardiac arrest tray. At the rate he was going there would be no trays left for subsequent arrests. He knew that he was wasting precious seconds but he felt that he was getting nowhere anyway - he had to try something. As calmly as he could he drew the solution into a syringe and slid the needle into the patient's vein. After what seemed like an eternity, although it was probably only seconds, the screen on the ECG monitor flickered as the man's heart started to beat again. But, as suddenly as it had restarted, the screen returned to it's flat green line again. Pip drew up another injection and punctured the man's vein yet again. The arm would be badly bruised - if he lived. The screen burst into life again and after a few seconds settled down into a steady rhythm. When he was sure that it would continue Pip gave a sigh of relief and flopped down into a chair at the bedside. For a few moments he had begun to doubt his expertise and wonder if he was doing something wrong.

Suddenly a terrible though struck him. He hadn't done something wrong. The drugs on the cardiac arrest trays hadn't worked, yet those in the cupboard had. What if the drugs on the trays were faulty. If it was a faulty batch they could be on every cardiac arrest tray in the hospital. He had to do something before they were needed again. Pip ran down the corridor to the duty nursing officer's room. Miss Sven was sitting behind her desk speaking to a student nurse as Pip barged through the door.

"Doctor Barton. What's the meaning of this. Can't you see that I'm busy. Don't you know that it's manners to knock before entering a room. " shouted Miss Sven as she glowered at him, which seemed to be the most common look that resided on her face.

"There's a problem with the cardiac arrest trays. I think that some of the drugs on them are faulty. One patient has died already and another almost did. We have to get the rest of the trays in the hospital checked."

As he recounted what had happened in the previous half hour the blood visibly drained from the nursing officer's face as she realised the possible enormity of the problem that they were faced with. There were over fifty trays scattered throughout the hospital, not to mention those that were normally kept in the coronary care unit. The only people who had records of where all the trays were, and who would be able to tell if the faulty batch was on the trays was pharmacy. And it was closed ! Why did these problems always happen at the weekend. The nursing officers had keys to get into the pharmacy, but she hadn't a clue where to start looking for the records. She quickly picked up the telephone and dialled the switchboard.

"It's Miss Sven here. can you page the on-call pharmacist for me. I'm in my office. All right, you can go now" she said, turning to the nurse "I'll speak to you later."

Now they had to wait. There was always a delay trying to contact someone outside the hospital. Even when they answered their page there was no guarantee that they would be in the vicinity of the hospital. Pip and Miss Sven sat opposite each other in the office, each wrapped up in their own thoughts.

What if he had acted rashly? Maybe he had been at fault after all and there was nothing wrong with the drugs. He was going to look very foolish if he was wrong and had visions of his career in tatters.

His thoughts were interrupted by the sudden burr from the telephone. From the one side of the conversation that he could hear he presumed the caller to be the on-call pharmacist. A few moments later Miss Sven returned the receiver to its cradle.

"You may have gathered that that was the pharmacist. She will be here in fifteen minutes. If you can tell her what drugs appear to be faulty then she can check her records and find out if they are on any other trays in the hospital."

"Appear to be faulty. You think that it may be me who is at fault."

Dispense With Death

"No that's not what I meant, and I'm sorry for snapping at you."

"That's all right. You weren't to know why I barged into your office. I would have done the same in your position. Let's just keep our fingers crossed that there aren't any more arrests before we get this all sorted out."

Pip picked up a nursing journal that was lying on the desk.

"May I?"

"Go ahead."

Anything would do to pass the time until the pharmacist arrived. He tried to concentrate on an article about nursing infants in Bangladesh but found himself unable to. What was keeping her? A glance at his watch told him the answer. It was only two minutes since the phone call. The next twenty minutes dragged by like a dredger making its way up a silted city river. Eventually there was a knock at the door.

"Sorry I took so long."

Pip turned round to see a young girl standing in the doorway, dressed in sweatshirt and jeans. He assumed that she was the pharmacist.

"I got held up in traffic. There's a football match on and the traffic is being controlled by the police and traffic wardens. You know how that causes traffic jams."

Yes, he had noticed an article about the match in the paper. It was a big charity affair. He had wanted to go, but he hadn't been able to swap his shift. Now he wished that he was stuck in the traffic going to the match. It would be infinitely better than sitting here in this office with its bare, antiseptic, pale green, walls. Waiting.

The girl introduced herself as Helene Smith. Miss Sven gave her a brief rundown on what had occurred, with Pip filling in details when he got the chance.

"How long do you reckon that it will take you to check your records?" Pip asked.

"Checking the records shouldn't take too long - about five minutes or so once I get into the pharmacy. There's only a problem if the batch of drugs that you had a problem with is on any other trays throughout the hospital. Do you know the batch number of the drugs?"

"The batch number? I never thought to look. The empty vials are in the 'sharps' disposal bin in the wards. As I said it was only after the second incident that I thought that there might be a problem with the drugs."

"Do you know what numbers the trays were?"

"No, but they'll still be on the wards."

"That's all right then. If I know the tray number then I can find out the batch number from our records and then take it from there."

"Would it help if we came down to pharmacy with you?" said Miss Sven.

"It wouldn't make much  "

Dispense With Death

Pip interrupted before she could finish "Let's all go down now. I couldn't bear to sit around here for any longer not knowing what's happening."

All three of them headed out of the office and down the corridor towards the pharmacy. As always seemed to be the case it was situated in the basement of the building.

"Doesn't it frighten you if you have to come in here late at night?"

"Only if I get called out for the burglar alarm. Then I make sure that one of the porters is with me if I arrive before the police. It can be a bit spooky, especially with the odd creaks and groans that you get from the equipment. I just switch on every light switch that I pass."

They had now arrived at the pharmacy. Helene switched off the burglar alarm and headed towards the dispensary with Pip and Miss Sven following behind. In no time Helene had located the cardiac arrest tray record book.

"Oh my God! That batch number you used is on virtually every tray in the hospital."

"How many is that ?" asked Pip.

"Sixty eight, including the three that you used. It'll take all afternoon to change them."

Helene quickly divided the hospital into six areas. Each of the areas had at least one tray that was all right.

"If we concentrate on one area at a time and get the suspect trays back to change over the drugs, then we can still leave cover in the event of an arrest. It won't be much, but in the circumstances it's the best that we can do."

Three hours later two porters left the pharmacy with the last lot of trays. There was a pile of vials lying on the dispensary bench.

"I'm glad that's over" sighed Helene. "There's nothing more that we can do until Monday morning. I'll contact the drug company then and we'll take it from there."

Tom delivered the tray back to the ward. So much for the Saturday afternoon shift being quiet. For the past two and a half hours he and Gavin Harvey had been running back and forth between pharmacy and virtually every ward in the hospital. Something was going on but they hadn't been able to find out what. The pharmacy was supposed to be closed on Saturday afternoons, not busier than it was during the week. At least he could get the story from Becky - she could ask her new boyfriend.

"That's your tray returned Sister" said Tom, as he entered the duty room. "Yours is the last one to be changed. Do you know what this is all about?"

"All I was told was not to use my tray until it had been replaced, because of a problem with the drugs. I'm just glad that we didn't need to use it this afternoon."

"That seems to be the story on every ward, with some variations. No-one seems to know the whole story, so people add on what they think has happened. There will be all sorts of rumours flying around within a couple of days unless someone comes out with the truth."

Dispense With Death

"If it's something really serious I doubt if we will ever find out the whole truth. There will be a version of the truth put out to stop tongues wagging. But you can bet it will be a sanitised version, scrubbed cleaner than a surgeon before an operation, with no blame attached to anyone. After all we can't have the general public losing faith in their local hospital. If it's something trivial then we'll know very soon. The length of time before someone high up makes a statement will give you an idea of how serious it was."

"Isn't that a very cynical view?"

"Maybe. But I've seen it all before, though not in this hospital. Years ago, there was this consultant who was a bit fond of a tipple, often before an operation. Now that was fine, as long as nothing went wrong. But one day he had just a drop too much, made a wrong incision and a woman bled to death on the operating table. That never came out and those present, including myself, helped to cover it up. Of course he couldn't be allowed to continue in post and was quietly retired early, the official reason being 'family reasons', although he lost not a penny piece of his pension. Maybe things are different now, but I doubt it."

## Chapter 5

Monday morning again. The weekends seemed too short. Admittedly he had made it shorter by doing a locum on Saturday, but the extra cash came in handy. 8.30. Shit! He was late. Ben jumped out of bed and ran to the bathroom. He threw some water at his face, more to waken him up than anything else, and dressed as quickly as he could. He ran down the stairs and got into the car. Start, come on damn you, start. At the fourth turn of the key the engine coughed and spluttered into life, like a sixty fags a day man drawing his first breath in the morning. Ben slammed the gears into first and shot down the road. Two blasts on the horn almost gave the old man in a Lada a heart attack, as Ben sped past him. Stupid old goat, dithering along at 30 when people were trying to get to work. Ben skidded to a halt in the parking lot, narrowly missing his boss's new car in the process. that would be all he needed. As he walked into the department Helene was standing checking one of the ward drug orders.

"Late again Ben. You had better watch that Miss McLean doesn't catch you. Did you have a good weekend?"

"Not bad. What about you?"

"Well apart from spending Saturday afternoon in here I had a great weekend."

"How come?"

Helene proceeded to recount the tale to Ben.

"So what happens now?"

"We have to wait and see what the company say. On Saturday night I decided it was too important to wait until this morning so I tried to contact someone at the company. Eventually at eleven o'clock I got a hold of their Quality Control manager. He arranged for one of those speedy delivery services to pick up the vials yesterday and now we just have to wait."

"Any ideas what went wrong?"

"The initial thought is that it is a sub-potent batch. Unfortunately we don't have the vials that the doctor used as he had finished the vials and put them in the sharps bin. I've never seen such commotion around here - one patient dead and the other only saved by Dr. Barton's quick thinking."
Just then one of the technicians interrupted them.

"Helene, that's the 'phone for you in the lab."

"Okay. Look, I'll see you later Ben."

"Yeah. Let me know what happens."

"That was the drug company on the 'phone. They've tested every vial that we sent back to them and they say that they are all right. there's nothing wrong with the drugs."

D just recently taken up his post as consultant in charge of the psychogeriatric unit in the hospital. With his dark good looks it was easy to believe that he came from Spain, as was stated on his passport. But he had no Spanish connection whatsoever. His passport, like all the other papers he carried, were forgeries. Forgeries of the highest calibre, gathered over the years, just in case. Four months previously he had been grateful for the forward planning when the papers had to be pressed hurriedly into use as he fled his South American homeland.

As chief medical officer for the military junta Hermes had wielded enormous power. When the country had returned to democracy he knew that it would not be safe for him to remain. His enemies would ensure that his life expectancy would be less than that of a snowball in the summer sun. Hermes had been responsible for torturing, and experimenting with drugs on, hundreds of "enemies of the state". The worst crime that most of his victims had been guilty of was to have been in the wrong place at the wrong time.

He recalled the good times before the recent free elections. The military governor had held a plebiscite the previous year, in the misguided belief that it would reinforce his authority. Instead it had had the opposite effect and set in motion the train of events that had culminated in the recent free election and the appointment of a left wing civilian, Javier Collor, as President. At least General Boas had had the foresight to change the constitution allowing him to remain commander-in-chief of the army for another five years.

There was still hope that the military could retake power and he could return home.

The new regime had decided that the image of the country had to be cleaned up in the eyes of the world. Already there were calls for those responsible for the torture and violent crimes, perpetrated in the name of the military junta, to be brought to justice, and that meant that people like Hermes had to go. Or at least Juan Hermes's previous incarnation had to go, for the name was taken from one of his 'patients' who had no further use for it. Even before the dust of the election had settled Hermes was on his way. A circuitous route, backtracking and laying false trails to prevent detection, had resulted in his arrival in Britain two months previously. Picking up a copy of 'The Times' at Heathrow he was surprised to see an article about himself on the front page. An official communique from the new junta stated that he had committed suicide in remorse for his crimes against humanity. Reading between the lines Hermes took it to mean that with him "officially dead" agents of the junta, and those sympathetic to it, could exact their retribution if they should come across him. After all - how could they be prosecuted for killing a dead man. Hermes knew that while the political situation in his country remained as it was he would have to watch his back. Commit suicide - never.

The one saving grace about the article was the lack of a photograph. Hermes had been very careful to avoid being photographed, even to the extent of developing his own passport photograph himself. He had stood over the forger as he prepared the passport and then burnt the negatives and unused photographs. The prospect of plastic surgery did not appeal to him, but would probably have been a necessity had he not taken such precautions. But when dealing with his own life no detail was too small. His other papers credited him with exceptional qualifications, enough to obtain a job anywhere. He had to admit that he was lucky to get this job so quickly. He had come financially prepared for a far longer period without a regular income.

The opportunity to experiment on the patients in his new unit was very tempting. Few of them received regular visitors and most were in such a confused state that more often than not they hadn't a clue what was happening to them. Of course he would have to considerably modify his methods - to be more subtle. No more of the treatment that he used back home. He would have to adapt to his new surroundings. Some of the drugs that were available in the hospital would come in useful, supplemented by others that he had brought with him when he fled - drugs that no normal hospital would stock.

Ward rounds had presented him with an ideal opportunity to assess the patients. Already he had earmarked three women for 'treatment'. If things went wrong and they died - who would know why? They were all over eighty years of age and could go at anytime as it was.

The morning round had just finished. This afternoon would be the time to start. He would break himself in gently to get the feel of the patients and the general situation in the unit.

"Did you hear about the excitement at the weekend Dr Hermes?"
Hermes had been miles away and the sister's question transported him back.
"What? Sorry"

Dispense With Death

"The problem with the drug trays. Surely you've heard about it?"

"No. I haven't been in the hospital at all this weekend. What happened?"

"Apparently a patient died because of a problem with the drugs on the emergency trays. At least that's the story that I've heard most often."

"What do you mean the story you've heard most often?"

"Well, in a hospital this size rumours and stories start very easily. Some people have been saying that the doctor is trying to cover up his mistakes and is putting the story around."

This put a new perspective on things. Perhaps today might not be a good day to start after all. If anything untoward should happen then it would direct attention onto him, and that was one thing that he didn't want.

"Where did all this happen?"

"Over in the medical wards, in the main building, on Saturday."

Far enough away to be almost totally separate from his unit. But.... no. He would wait for at least a day or two before commencing anything. Better to be safe than sorry.

"No point in letting it bother us, eh sister. After all we don't have a lot in common with the medical wards, do we?"

Ben was just leaving the pharmacy to do his rounds in the geriatric wards. Situated a mile away from the main hospital grounds they were a pleasant stroll away when the sun was shining. Today it wasn't. It was raining. Heavily. It was a day to travel to the wards by car.

The condensation on the windows and the water dripping in through the ill-fitting roof conspired to make the journey to the wards a slow and hazardous affair. Weather like this made Ben wish that he had opted for a closed sports car instead. The demister was fighting a losing battle with the encroaching dampness. Ben fished a disposable hat from his coat pocket to clear the screen. A rivulet of water ran down the inside of the windscreen. A wiper on the inside was what was needed in weather like this.

He parked the car and dashed into the ward. With any luck the nurses might take pity on him and offer him a cup of tea. Pushing open the swing doors a familiar sight and odour greeted him. It depressed him, as always. Old women moaning, looking for bed pans, and screens drawn around half the beds. The ward sister was sitting in the duty room, having her tea break. Ben deposited himself in an empty chair sending some samples, left by a sales rep, tumbling to the floor from the desk as he did so.

"Sorry Carol. Any chance of a cuppa?"

"Help yourself, after you pick those up" she said pointing at the mess on the floor.
"I hear that things are a bit hectic up at the pharmacy these days."

"Ah that's great" said Ben as he downed half a mug of tea in one go. "I needed that. Yeah, a bit of a flap over the weekend. You heard about it?"

"Uh huh. I think everybody has. One of the porters came and swapped over our cardiac arrest tray on Saturday. That's when we found out."

"Did you hear what they thought was wrong?"

"Someone mentioned faulty drugs."

"That was the original thought. But we've been in touch with the company and it would appear that the drugs are all right. So now no-one is any the wiser as to what happened. One rumour that I've heard doing the rounds is that the doctor made a mistake and is trying to cover it up."

"Surely not."

"I don't quite know whether to believe it myself. But it would fit in with all that we know just now."

"Who was the doctor?"

"A Doctor Barton, over in the Medical unit. I don't know whether it's really true, but I've heard of it happening before - a doctor makes a mistake under pressure and tries to cover it up. Even if the patient dies the initial mistake can be overlooked and the doctor will carry on in his job. The big crime is to try and cover the mistake up. If you're found out all hell breaks loose. If that has happened his career is up the spout. Not to mention any possible criminal charges that could be brought.

Anyway, I had better get on with some work. I can't sit here gossiping and drinking tea all day. People will wonder where I've got to."

Ben took the keys for the medicine cupboards and headed out towards the ward. As he entered the main ward he could just hear the sister repeating what they had been talking about to one of the other nurses. No wonder rumours spread quickly in the hospital.

## Chapter 7

Hermes sat in his penthouse flat, overlooking the river, reflecting on his first few days in a British hospital. How different it was to back home. Back home - he really had to stop thinking about there. Spain was home if anyone should ask. He could never return to his real homeland - at least not for the foreseeable future. He thought back to the old days. Then patients would be spirited away in the night to further his 'research'. No-one dared to complain lest the same fate befell them. That could never happen here. If he was to try that now there would be an uproar from the patient's relatives, to say the least. He could feel the desire inside him to continue in his old ways, but the voice of reason restrained him, advising him to formulate a more discreet method of treatment.

His favourite had been to test people's pain threshold. First of all he would mildly sedate the 'patient' to remove any feelings of anxiety that they had. Then an injection of his chosen painkiller was followed by a dousing with petrol. Once set alight he would time the period before the screams started. All his research had been carefully documented but had had to be destroyed before he fled the country. Incriminating evidence like that could not be kept lest it fall into the wrong hands. All that work lost. Of course he could not repeat experiments like that now. Possibly an injection of some irritant would have a similar effect.

He had to leave most of his personal belongings behind necessitating the purchase of a complete new wardrobe of clothes. However he had managed to take two suitcases with him. One contained money in various currencies, plus personal papers. The currency would have to be exchanged for British money, but over a period of time, in various widespread locations so as not to draw attention to the transactions. The papers were another matter. Those he would have to find a safe place for, because as well as his new forged documents there were papers giving his true identity which, for some inexplicable reason, he had found himself unable to dispose of. If those fell into the wrong hands his outlook was not good. A lot of people had cause to want him dead and would relish the opportunity if it arose. The second suitcase contained equally damaging evidence, although of a more substantial nature. The contents belied his role as a man of mercy and compassion. These were the tools of his real trade. All sorts of instruments of torture ranging from the surgeon's scalpel to items that he had designed and built himself. The mouth gag to stifle screams, but with the addition of an inner, rotating, blade which could be used once a gag was in place. The capsules, each half of which contained a chemical. The action of stomach acid on the gelatine shell resulted in an explosive mixture of the two chemicals. A roll of fine steel thread which formed a lethal garrotte. These, and others, were unlikely to be of use to him now, but again he couldn't bring himself to leave them behind.

He slid both cases under the bed. Until a more suitable place could be found for them they would be safe there. Mrs Molcodas, his domestic, might moan about them, but she would never dare move them, let alone look inside them. Opening the drawer of his writing desk Hermes removed his passport. That miserable Egyptian had thought his life would be spared if he prepared the false documents for the doctor. With that in mind he had taken great care over their preparation and even the most niggardly Customs officer would have great difficulty in distinguishing them from the genuine article. When the job was completed and he had the documents safe Hermes had called the forger into his office and told him that he would no longer be kept prisoner, and that he was free to go. With a great show of thanks the man had headed for the door. Just as he pulled it open Hermes withdrew his gun from the desk drawer and shot the man, once, in the back of the head. Hermes felt that he was doing the man a favour - a quick, painless death. And of course it eliminated the one person who knew that Hermes's documents were false.

Placing his wallet beside the passport Hermes closed the drawer. His mind ran forward to tomorrow. He would have to start the planning for further experiments, but cover them up in the routine running of the unit. He started turning over the possibilities in his head, committing nothing to paper for the present.

## Chapter 8

At midnight the canteen was virtually deserted. A doctor and two nurses were the only other there when Tom walked in. He had been on night shift now for a week and a half. Things were certainly a lot quieter than during the day. All the labs were closed and the hospital ticked over waiting for another busy day to start. The only excitement so far had been when an elderly patient had 'discharged' herself in the middle of the night and Tom and another porter were dispatched to catch her before she made it out the main gates. Apart from that he had spent most of the time reading. At least now he was being paid to do it - better than being on the dole and reading anything to pass the time. As he left the servery he noticed that the doctor was now on his own. Tom decided to join him at the table. One good thing about the hospital at night was how much more friendly people were - like a small village compared with the bustling city that was the hospital in daytime.

Sitting in the canteen at midnight was not his idea of fun but Pip couldn't face going to bed just yet. He had spent the last two hours stopping people from vomiting and helping them to get to sleep. Now he was still wide awake and thirsty. The coffee wouldn't help him to sleep but it would slate his thirst. It was now two weeks since the incident with the trays and officially he had heard no more other than that the drugs returned to the company had been all right. Unofficially he had heard that he was being blamed and a multitude of rumours were circulating the hospital about the incident.

"Hello doctor. Mind if I join you?"

Pip looked up to see a porter standing at the table. He was sure that he recognised him, but wasn't sure where from. "No No. Go ahead."

"Quiet around here at this time of night."

"Yes. First time I've been in here at this time. Usually I'll just have a cuppa in my room if I'm on call but tonight I just had to get away from there. You working the night shift?"

"Yes. I'll drink this and head back to the porter's room. There's not much happening at this time of night so we have to fill in our time as best we can."

"You're lucky. I'll be glad to grab a few minutes sleep tonight. It's so unpredictable - some nights you're kept going all the time, others you might just have to get up the once."

Both men finished off their coffees. As Pip's room was close to the porter's room they decided to accompany each other through the grounds.

"Aren't you the doctor who was involved in all that fuss a couple of weeks back?"
Pip groaned. He had lost count of the number of times he had been asked that same question.

"Yes."

"What really happened ? I was on that day and spent all the afternoon running between different wards and the pharmacy exchanging trays."

That was where he recognised him from. Pip told him his version of events and had just finished as they entered the medical block. Suddenly their path was blocked by a young nurse.

"Dr. Barton. I thought I heard your voice. Come quickly. Mrs Darents has just collapsed on the floor."

Both men ran into the ward to find a middle aged woman lying flat out in the middle of the floor. Pip recognised the woman as the one he had been examining less than an hour ago. What had he done now!

Carefully, they lifted her up onto her bed and Pip began examining her.

"There doesn't appear to be any damage from the fall. What happened?"

"Just after you left I gave her the painkillers you prescribed. About five minutes ago she went to the toilet. When she came out she almost made it to her bed and then she fell. I suppose I panicked a bit, but I heard your voice. That's when you came in."

"She's asleep"

"What?"

"She's asleep. She didn't collapse. Did you give her any night sedation? I just gave her two of the capsules you prescribed."

"Capsules? What I prescribed only comes as a tablet. Let me see the bottle you used."

The nurse quickly ran to the medicine trolley and picked out the bottle of painkillers.

Dispense With Death

"It was a new bottle that I had to open to give her her medication. I checked the label carefully."

Pip took the bottle from her and examined it. True enough it was the painkillers that he had prescribed. But they wouldn't have caused any sedation. He was just about to put the bottle back down when he remembered the nurse's comment about capsules. He took the lid off the bottle and tipped some of the contents into his hand. The bright orange capsules stared back up at him.

"These aren't painkillers, they're sleeping pills. Look. You were right - the label is correct. It's what's inside the bottle that's wrong."

Pip felt a great sense of relief wash over him. He had had visions of having to go through the hell of the past two weeks again. This time it definitely was not his fault. The bottle had been packed in the hospital pharmacy - it was someone there who was at fault.

"What do we do now?"

"Well at this time hopefully no-one else will need analgesia and if they do I'll make sure that I use another drug. Even if they do get a sedative instead I don't suppose that it'll do much harm. I'll get in touch with the pharmacy tomorrow. I mean today. I'm off to bed. Don't worry. I'll sort it out."

"Is Miss McLean in?"

It was 8.30 and the pharmacy had just opened. Pip had decided that the best course of action was to go straight to the top. After all the mistake could have had much more serious consequences. Just then Val McLean walked out of her office. Still only 27 her career had sky rocketed and had taken over as Principal Pharmacist six months previously.

"Dr Barton. What can I do for you?"

"I'd rather speak to you in your office, if you don't mind."

"No problem. Come on through."

Pip walked through into the office and sat down. Sitting at the wrong side of a desk was getting to be a habit. At least this time he was definitely sure that he was in the right.

"It's not about the trays again, is it?"

"No, this is another problem. One that happened early this morning. Have a look at these."

Taking the bottle from his pocket Pip placed it on the desk. As Val McLean examined it Pip related his tale.

"Now I know that I will probably be accused of trying to put the blame on someone else. Again. But as you can see the label and the contents don't tie up.

Have you any idea how it happened?"

"Someone else saw this?"

"Yes the nurse on the ward."

"And you took the bottle away with you?"

"Yes, I didn't want anyone else receiving the wrong medicine. What are you implying?"

"Nothing. I'm just getting my facts straight. I'll have to check into this. At least we should be able to trace the bottle back through our system easily enough and find out what happened. Can I get back to you and let you know?"

"How long?"

"This afternoon, at the latest. I'll try for sooner. We'll have to check that there's no more of these around in the hospital. I'll call you when I find out something. What's your bleep number?"

"371. And you'll check out those trays again, in case they're related to this?"

"Yes. Okay."

She showed him out and sat back down at her desk, staring at the bottle in front of her. When Dr. Barton had shown her the bottle she had recognised the initials of the pharmacist who had checked it, but had said nothing. She had had her doubts about the man for a couple of months and there had been rumours that he had a drink problem. To make a mistake like this could have had terrible consequences. And if he had been involved in checking those trays .... At least she could be fairly certain that there were not a lot of bottles of these tablets around. it wasn't a drug that was used very often and it was only packed down from it's original large container when a ward required it. First of all a quick check of the cardiac arrest trays was in order before she took matters further.

Dispense With Death

Fortunately the records showed that Paul hadn't been involved with any of the three suspect trays, which came as a great relief to her. That just left the problem of the capsules. She would have to bring in the human resources officer, if she was to do things properly. She did not like to do it, but it had to be done. The ill feeling that would undoubtedly result couldn't be helped. She picked up the telephone, called human resources and arranged a meeting for that afternoon. Now she would have to tell Paul. She couldn't just spring the meeting on him. Before she did that she decided to phone Dr Barton - unfortunately for his peace of mind there wasn't an easy culprit to blame for the trays.

"I wasn't here on that day. It couldn't possibly have been me."

"It's your signature on the bottle. Look."

"It's my writing, but I didn't write it. I'm telling you I wasn't here on that day. I was on a weeks holiday. Check the leave calendar and you'll see that."

Val got out of her seat and looked at the calendar she kept on the office wall to keep track of who was off on holiday. Oh my God! The old man was right. He had been off on holiday. She remembered it now. He had talked about it for weeks beforehand. His brother had invited him down to the south coast for a weeks sailing. What was she going to do now?

"I remember it now. I'm sorry. But you can see that it looks like your signature."

"Well it's either someone's idea of a joke, or someone is out to get me. I know what they all think of me. You included."

Val felt her face turn crimson.

"And don't try to deny it. You all think that I'm a doddering old bumbler who finds refuge in a whisky bottle at night. No doubt when you saw the container you thought 'Oh no, not another of his mistakes'. Well you're wrong. And I want something done about it. Now."

He was right, of course. That was what she had been thinking. But things were very different now. This may have started out as a bit of tomfoolery by someone, but it had become totally out of hand. Someone could have been seriously injured - almost was. And the reputation of the department would be shot to hell.

"I agree. This is totally ridiculous. First of all I really am very sorry. You can see why I called you in. Can't you?"

"Yes. In truth I would have done the same in your position. I know that I make the odd mistake, but who doesn't. But this definitely was not one of them."

"No-one else in the department knows about this yet. The doctor only handed the bottle in fifteen minutes ago. And you have my word that this conversation won't be repeated, to anyone. I'll have to contact the hospital administrator about this, but first I want to speak to all the staff and see if I can shame the culprit into owning up. Can you gather everyone together in the staff room in ten minutes. Just tell them that I have an announcement to make. Don't say what it's about."

When he had left the room Val picked up the phone. This was a problem she had never had to face before and she needed some guidance. The meeting with human resources this afternoon was going to be totally different to what she had originally intended.

"Last night a woman collapsed in one of the wards. This department was the direct cause of her collapse. She had been given a sedative from a bottle that was supposed to contain analgesics. If that had been the only problem. a wrongly labelled bottle, it would be bad enough. Any mistake that gets out of this department reflects badly on everyone.. But this was not a mistake. It was a deliberate act. Someone, one of you, put another person's name on the bottle - no doubt thinking that it would be good for a giggle - to make that person look bad. Well it's not funny. That patient could have been badly injured, or even died."

No-one said a word. And no-one looked as if they were about to own up.

"If no-one owns up now then admin. have said that it will be a police matter. Even if the culprit owns up then there's no guarantee that the police will not be involved but it would spare everyone else a lot of unpleasantness."

Silence. She thought that one of the pharmacists had been about to say something, but she couldn't be sure.

"Right. You leave me no option but to have admin. call in the police. You can all go back to your jobs for the moment, but each one of you can expect to be called in to my office. I'm sure that the police will want to interview all of you individually."

Dispense With Death

With that Val turned and headed back to her office. She had been sure that the threat to involve the police would have made the guilty party own up. Perhaps they had been too frightened to do so in public. The call to the administrator could wait fifteen minutes.

Twenty five minutes later Val realised that no-one was going to own up and that she would have to make the call. At least she wouldn't be the one calling the police - that unpleasant duty would be left to the hospital administrator.

It was the afternoon before the police arrived. In the meanwhile Dr Barton had been back on to find out what was happening. When Val told him he suggested a horrendous possibility - what if the same person had done the same thing to the cardiac trays and substituted something else, maybe water, instead of the active drugs. That would explain their lack of action. Val was taken aback at the suggestion, feeling that he was going over the top about the trays, but agreed that it was a possibility. Paul's signature wasn't on the faulty trays which seemed to rule it out, especially if someone had switched the capsules to get at him, but she would have to mention it to the police.

Detective Inspector Angus Critchley had risen quickly through the ranks. He had been picked out as one of the 'future hopes' of the force when he was doing his training and had never looked back. He did, however, hold some unorthodox views. He eschewed what he classed as 'boring' police transport, preferring instead to use his own car. There had been opposition but he had won through in the end. The fact that his car was a Lotus Esprit Turbo had raised eyebrows higher still, but he still got away with it.

His father had made his fortune after the war, although no-one seemed to know exactly how. He had one son, Angus, who had wanted for nothing. A career in the police was the last job Angus would have been expected to pursue, but when he turned round on his seventeenth birthday and told his parents that that was what he wanted to do they knew that there was no point in arguing with him.

His rapid rise to his present position at the age of 35, combined with his extravagant lifestyle, had made him few friends amongst his colleagues but few could deny his prowess as a policeman.

Finding a fixing point for the detachable blue light on the roof of the Lotus had been a problem. The light was magnetic and the car body was made from GRP. The bonding of a small metal plate under the headlining had solved that problem. One advantage of the light was that he could exploit the car's considerable performance on Britain's speed restricted highways.

He drew into the hospital grounds and parked the car. As he got out he turned to see his partner struggling to get his leg over the wide sill. This was only DC Coll's second day with him and he had yet to master the art of entering and exiting the car.

"You should be glad that you don't wear a skirt Norman. That's a most inelegant pose that you're striking."

"It's the car. I'm not used to getting into something as low as this."

"You will. Let's go in and see if we can get this problem sorted out sharpish."

"Miss McLean? I'm Detective Inspector Critchley and this is my colleague, Detective Constable Coll. We were just given a brief outline of the case at the station. Perhaps you could fill in the details?"

Val recounted what had occurred, leaving out only Dr Barton's latest suggestion.

"Well it looks as if we will have to talk to each staff member. Do you have a list of their names and we could work through them?"

"Yes, you could use this fire roll call list."

"Good. Nineteen staff. Hopefully we can clear it up today. It's a messy business and the quicker it's over with the better for all concerned. Is everyone here today?"

"Yes. I think so. You could leave Paul Bennet out though. He's the one who seems to have been the victim of all this."

"We'll interview him all the same. Just to get his story. Can we use your office?"

"By all means. Go ahead. I'll just be next door if you need me."

"If you don't mind I'd like to begin with you. I realise that you called us in but we have to interview everyone. I hope you understand."

"Yes. Yes. Of course."

"Right. What's the system for checking things?"

"Well, everything is sealed with a snap on sealing lid so that we can tell if it has been opened should it come back from a ward. And the final check is always carried out by a pharmacist."

"And how easy would it be to tamper with a seal?"
"Well I suppose someone could always remove a lid and replace it with a new sealed one. But Paul.."

"Mr Bennet?"

"Yes. But Mr Bennet wasn't here on the date that the label states that the bottle was packed on, so it's unlikely to have been altered in that way."

"Could it have been packed and not checked for a few days? Then it would be possible that he may have checked it?"

"I suppose it's possible although we do try to have everything cleared away at night-time. I had thought of that as well, but it was right in the middle of his holiday. It's highly unlikely that it would have lain about for so long without someone checking it. That would be the most satisfactory outcome though."

"What do you mean?"

"Well - a simple mistake. Nothing sinister behind it. No need to involve you further."

"Mmm. Yes, I see." Angus was silent.

"Well that's all I require from you for the moment. I'll have a word with the others. I'll just take them in the order that they are on this list. Let me see now. Can you ask Mr. Brosan to come in?"

Ben couldn't help noticing the car. After all it was parked next to his. Next to the Lotus his Triumph Spitfire looked what it was - old and cheap. The cars that the police drove about in these days! As he drove down the main driveway he noticed Becky heading towards the gate.

"Do you want a lift home?"

Becky turned round to find Ben's car stopped beside her.

"Hi. Yeah, that would be great. I've been on my feet all day and they're killing me."

"So you're not up to going out tonight?"

"Oh I don't know. If I'm asked nicely I just might. Look, why don't you come for tea. I'm sure that my parents won't mind."

Ben turned left out the gate and headed in the general direction of Becky's house.

"If you're sure that it's no trouble"

"No trouble. Well now that's settled how was your day?"

"Oh, apart from being interviewed by the police, it was just the same as normal."

"Interviewed by the police!"

"Yes. Apparently this woman collapsed last night on one of the wards. It turned out that a bottle of tablets was wrongly labelled and she was given the wrong medication. According to the bottle it was checked by old Paul Bennet, but he denies it saying that someone did it to make a fool of him and that it had gone too far. Val called in the police as no-one would own up to it. Personally, I wouldn't be surprised if Paul had made a mistake - it wouldn't be the first time."

"What did the police do?"

"Yours truly got hauled in first, probably because I'm first on the roll call. I hope."

"What sort of questions did they ask you?"

"First they asked did I do it. Of course I said no. Even if I had do they think that I would own up on the first question. Then they asked if I knew anyone who might have. Did I know anyone who disliked Paul enough to do this. So I told them. No. That I thought Paul had most likely done it himself."

They were stuck in the rush hour traffic. Ben hated driving in these conditions. It was so boring and he got so frustrated. Up ahead he could see a blue flashing light. As he got closer he could see the badly dented remains of a car whose driver obviously hadn't been looking where he was going. It only served to make the congestion worse. Ben spotted a gap and shot down a side street. Knowing the short cuts at least cut out some of the hassles. It also meant that he could get above crawling speed and clear of the fog of diesel fumes that a taxi had kindly belched into his car.

Dispense With Death

"Bloody taxis. If they're not turning in front of you without indicating they're trying some other method of doing you in."

"How long were you in for?"

"In where?"

"With the police."

"Oh. about fifteen minutes. They have to come back tomorrow because they didn't manage to see everyone today."

"What'll happen after that?"

"It depends. If Paul made a mistake then he's going to look pretty stupid. What'll happen then is anybody's guess. On the other hand, if someone did do it, even for a joke, I wouldn't like to be in their shoes. The least that they can expect is the sack."

Ben slowed the car." This is your house, isn't it?"

As he pulled into the side of the street spots of rain started to fall. He quickly raised the roof and then ran up the path after Becky. He noticed the middle-aged woman picking up her garden tools.

"Mum. This is Ben. Remember I told you about him. You don't mind if he stays for tea, do you?"

"Hello, Mrs Donaldson. I hope it isn't putting you to too much trouble, but Becky insisted."

"Yes, she can be like that. And no, it's no trouble at all. Nice to meet you Ben.
Come on inside before the rain gets any heavier."

Ben was sure that he had seen the man sitting by the fire somewhere before, but he couldn't place him.

"Ben, this is my dad."

"Hello. Haven't we met before?"

"We might have passed in the hospital. I just started there a few weeks ago."

"That'll be it. I thought I knew your face."

Meeting Becky's parents had gone better than he had expected. He had been a bit nervous but hadn't told her. She would have just told him not to be silly. And she would have been right. After dinner they had gone out to the pictures and then for a drink. The afternoon's experience with the police, of which he had made light with Becky, was now almost forgotten.

Something wasn't right. He wasn't sure what, but his instinct told him that someone had been holding back information. There was still another four staff to question tomorrow morning. He would have preferred to have finished today and then thought it over tonight if no-one had owned up. As it was it would drag on for another day. Most of those he had spoken to stated that, in their opinion, Paul Bennet had made a mistake and didn't realise it. The man was obviously not very popular. As he turned the thoughts over in his head Angus Critchley powered the Lotus through the country lanes that would take him home. 'A good driver should be able to concentrate on other things as he drives. The car should be a part of him, an extension of his body' was his oft repeated maxim whenever he had a new officer in the car with him. The fact that he drove one of the best handling cars in the world helped, as did the fact that he had dabbled in motor racing as a teenager. Some would say that he still dabbled in it, only this time on the public highway. He really would have to get back on a racetrack to see if he still had it in him.

The case would keep until tomorrow. Tonight he had a date with a former model. It may have been nearly ten years since she had last shown off her body in the newspapers, but the passage of time had looked favourably upon her not inconsiderable charms. A quick shower, shave, change of clothes and twenty five minutes later Angus was heading back through the lanes. A sudden crackle from the radio interrupted his thoughts. More yobbos causing trouble. Angus switched the set off. Tonight he was off duty.

## Chapter 9

8.30am. Reluctantly Angus dragged himself out of the unfamiliar bed. Last night was still fresh in his memory. It had been 4am before he had got to sleep. Susie lay motionless beside him, the curves of her body visible under the single satin sheet. Suppressing his rising feelings Angus turned on the shower and stepped under the ice cold water. Sheer hell, but guaranteed to wake him up. Five minutes later he stepped out of the shower to find Susie sitting up in bed, the sheet pulled up around her neck.

"Come back to bed."

"I can't. I have to be at work in twenty five minutes."

Angus dressed quickly trying to ignore the slowly slipping sheet in front of him.

"I'll phone you later."

Taking the steps two at a time he ran out to the car. Fifteen minutes was pushing it to reach the station, where Norman would be waiting for him.

Twenty minutes later the Lotus pulled into the station car park. Angus parked in his reserved space. The morning rush hour traffic hadn't been too bad. If truth be told he was only late because of last night, not the traffic. He pushed the memory to the back of his mind. Norman was standing there, waiting.

"Right Norman. Let's go. Hopefully we can get this hospital business wrapped up today. Have you any thoughts on it.

"Well, I had a few ideas" replied Norman as he fell into the car. "How long does it take to get the knack of getting into this?"

"You'll get used to it eventually. Now what have you come up with?"

"Well all of those that we spoke to yesterday seem to think that it is a genuine mistake, but Mr Bennet is adamant that it isn't. I can't see everyone involved in a conspiracy against him. At least not to that extent. So that would point to a genuine mistake."

"But."

"But, we haven't interviewed everyone yet and one of those may give us a different lead."

"Very good. It doesn't do to make a decision without all the facts. It may be that he does make a lot of mistakes and people don't want to believe that someone could do something like this. If someone has it's unlikely that they'll flee the country if they think we're on to them.

The first interview of the morning was with one of the younger technicians. All her answers checked out. As she left the room Angus turned to DC Coll.

"What do you think?"

"She sounded nervous, but then being interviewed by the police would account for that. There was something, but I couldn't quite figure out what it was." There was a knock at the door and another of the technicians came in.

"Sit down Miss Isaacs. I'm sure that you know why you're here. We just want to ask you a few questions. I'm Detective Inspector Critchley and this is Detective Constable Coll. You were working on the date that the alleged incident took place?"

"Yes."

"And did you notice anything unusual ?"

"No."

"Was Mister Bennet working that day?"

"I don't remember. He may have been. It's difficult to remember who's here and who isn't."

"What do you think of Mister Bennet?"

""What do you mean?"

"As a pharmacist."

"He seems to make a lot of mistakes."

"More than the other pharmacists?"

"Yes."

"And what happens about them?"

"Nothing."

"Nothing. You mean no-one bothers about them?"

Dispense With Death

"Well, people sometimes point out the mistakes to him. Other times they remedy them themselves to save any bother."

"And do you think that's right?"

"No."

"You think he should be disciplined about them?"

"Yes. Everyone else is. A lot of his mistakes aren't too bad but this is his worst, putting temazepam in the bottle instead of "

The girl stopped.

"Go on."

"Nothing. It was a bad mistake."

"How do you know that it was temazepam?"

"I assume that's what it was."

"It seemed more like a statement of fact to me. Miss McLean only mentioned that it was a sedative, not its name. You put the wrong capsules into the bottle, knowing that it would be blamed on Mister Bennet."

"No, that's not true."

"What were you hoping, that someone would be hurt and that something would have to be done about him?"

"No, it wasn't like that. I didn't mean for it to go this far."

The girl broke down. DC Coll left the room, returning moments later with Val McLean.

"Miss McLean" said Angus "I think we have our culprit."

"Mary, how could you?"

"Tell Miss McLean why you did it Mary" interrupted Angus

"I didn't mean for anyone to get hurt Miss McLean. Honest, I didn't. I was sure someone would notice the mistake even if it got to a ward. Most of Mister Bennet's mistakes are covered up, so you don't get to hear about them. I thought that you would be bound to hear about this and that something would be done about it. I never meant for it to turn out like this."
While Norman had been taking down the details Angus had radioed the station to send a car. A full statement could be taken there. The Lotus having only two seats made it difficult to transport suspects.

"No I'm sure you didn't" said Val "You realise that you'll probably lose your job, in addition to whatever happens with the police."

"That will depend" said Angus as he clipped the radio back into his pocket. "You know Mary, if Mister Bennet hadn't made a mistake when he originally packed down the tablets you might have got away with it. He put the wrong date on the bottle, a date that he wasn't here on. So, when this happened and the holiday rota showed that he was off on that date, his story gained some credence."

Dispense With Death

"See I told you" sobbed Mary "He's always making mistakes. Why wont you do something about him before it's too late."

## Chapter 10

"Sister, it's Miss McLean from pharmacy here. Do you know where I can contact Dr. Barton?"

"You've just missed him. He's gone along to the doctor's room."

"Right, thanks."

Val pressed the button to break the connection and dialled the doctor's room.

"Dr Barton? Hello, it's Val McLean here."

At last. He had been waiting for her call since yesterday.

"Have you discovered what happened?"

"Yes. All that I can say is that it was a mistake at our end and that it is now in the hands of the police. It's unlikely to happen again. How's the patient?"

"She's fine. None the worse for her experience. So it was a one off incident?"

"Yes. Someone being very stupid. I asked the girl if she had done anything else like this, not specifically mentioning the cardiac arrest trays, and she said no, that this was the first time. I must say that I believe her, she had nothing to gain by lying."

"Thanks. It's good to know that I wasn't at fault."

"I don't think that that was ever in doubt."

"Maybe not, but it's good to hear it confirmed anyway."

As he replaced the receiver Pip was still shocked. How could anyone have done anything so stupid? Unfortunately, or fortunately depending on the way that you looked at it, he was no nearer to finding an answer to the problem that had been nagging him for the past few weeks. To hell with it, he was off duty in half an hour. There was a golf match arranged with two of the surgical SHO's for the afternoon. At least the weather had stayed fine.

As he pulled into the main driveway he noticed the low slung Lotus Esprit in front. Some day, he mused. Some hope, on his pay.

Angus cut onto the motorway slip road and gunned the accelerator. Still in second gear the Lotus shot forward. Grabbing third gear they were soon travelling at over eighty miles an hour. A hold up necessitated an urgent stamp on the brakes. The car howled in protest as the disc brakes hauled it back down to a leisurely thirty miles an hour. Angus cursed. He had hoped for a clear road back to headquarters. He should have used the blue light. Too late for that now, they were well and truly enmeshed in the traffic. A fast drive cleared his mind and helped him to sort things out. And today he had a puzzle to solve. On the surface the case was closed, but there was something else there. He hadn't been told the whole story. Of that he was sure.

Pip drove into the golf course car park. Bill and Neil were already there waiting for him. Oh well, by the look of things they wouldn't have to hang around long before they could tee off. A group of four young lads were just about to head onto the first tee. Apart from that there was no-one else about.

The first boy stepped up to tee off. Straight up in the air and back down, travelling only about fifteen yards forward. His three friends fell about laughing. Pip couldn't believe it. If they were to be stuck behind this lot it would take all day, and that was just for the first hole.

The second lad lined up his tee shot. Sliced. Sharp right and only prevented from hitting the cars in the car park by the boundary wall. The other two tee shots followed similar wayward patterns. "Mind if we play through?" asked Neil as he strode onto the tee.

"Go ahead" replied lad two as he went to retrieve his ball.

Pip took all his frustrations out on the little white ball in front of him. Even though it was the wrong attitude to take to the shot he still managed to hit it a fair distance. Both Neil and Bill managed a few yards more. All three headed after their balls.

"How are things now over on the medical wards. Quietened down any?"

"You mean about the trays. Not too bad. No more excitement anyway. Still haven't got to the bottom of it. Doubt if I ever will. How are things with you?"

"So so. We've lost a few patients recently. We seem to be getting a run of really resistant infections."

"We've had that problem too" said Bill. "Even using the antibiotics recommended by bacteriology doesn't seem to help."

They were now on the first. Pip was faced with a twenty foot putt for a birdie four, and the hole. He lined it up carefully and struck it with the centre of the putter. The ball rolled straight and true and was heading for the hole, when two feet short, it suddenly deviated to the right.

"Unlucky"

"Unlucky my foot" stormed Pip "look at that hole. That's the problem with public courses. They let people on who have not got a clue about golf, like those four back there on the tee. Imagine doing that to the green."

"Pick up your ball and we'll call it a half. You're not getting the hole."
The rest of the round was incident free. As they came to the last tee all three had equal scores for the round.

"Ten pounds for the hole, and the round?" suggested Neil.

"Each?"

"Why not. twenty pounds to the winner. Five each if two of us tie."

Neil and Bill both hit reasonable drives, straight down the fairway. Pip teed up and addressed the ball. Relax, he tried to tell himself. His golf always seemed to go to pieces when he was under any pressure. Slowly he drew the club back and then swung through with all the force he could muster. At first the ball followed the

Dispense With Death

same trajectory as Bill and Neil's had, but then gradually began to fade to the right, ending up in the light rough. Damn it. Why couldn't he relax.

"Looks like my tenner's lost anyway."

"Don't be so hasty" said Bill. "It doesn't look too bad. You should get out of there easily."

When Pip reached the ball he could see that Bill was right - the lie was better than he had expected - in fact the ball was sitting up on a patch of newly cut grass. He took the five wood from his bag and hit the ball. This time it flew straight and true all the way, landing about forty yards short of the green. Following their second shots Neil's ball was about ten yards to the right of the green and Bill had overshot the green, landing in a bunker.

Neil lined up his shot. A little pitch should do it. Instead he stubbed the ground behind the ball, which then only travelled a matter of feet. Pip didn't want to make the same mistake. There was a bunker just in front of the green, right in his line to the flag. Should he be brave, or play safe. His decision made he played the shot. The ball looked to be heading for the bunker. Somehow it gained the legs to clear it. Two bounces later it was in the hole. He had won, unless Bill could pull off a great shot from the bunker. He couldn't, At last something had gone right for him.

"Your turn to buy the drinks Pip"

"Fine by me, but I'll be using your money to do it" replied Pip.

Dispense With Death

Tom had been transferred to day shift working in the surgical and orthopaedic wards. It was hard going, transferring patients between wards and theatre and vice versa. It also had its depressing side to it as well - he was in the process of wheeling his fifth body in three days down to the mortuary. This was an old lady of 85 who had broken her hip when she fell down stairs at home. She was in a bad way when she came in, suffering from hypothermia, in addition to the fracture. She had been lying behind the door of her flat all night before a neighbour found her in the morning. She had never seemed to make any progress and when complications set in she was too weak to fight through. For Tom his regular trip to the mortuary had changed his initial impression of Ron, the mortuary attendant, realising that he was not as unfeeling as first appeared. He pushed the trolley through the swing doors into the mortuary. No-one about.

"Hi Tom"

The voice belonged to Ron, who had just appeared from one of the side rooms.

"Hi Ron."

"That you bringing me more customers?"

"'Fraid so."

"That's the fifth one this week, isn't it? What are they doing up there - clearing out early for Christmas?"

"Don't start talking about Christmas already. I don't know what's going on. It seems that they've never had such a bad spell as this. You got any ideas?"

"Me? I just cut up the bodies. Well, actually most of the deaths are due to infection, but not always the same one. So that would tend to rule out an incumbent microorganism in the unit, like MRSA."

"What !!!"

"Sorry. I forgot that you're not up on the medical terms. MRSA? It's a germ that's present in some hospitals. The problem is that it is very difficult to kill. Most antibiotics don't work on it, and the few that do are very expensive. Once it gets into a unit it's very hard to get rid of it. Fortunately we don't have it here. But they may clean down the wards, just in case."

"Is it contagious?"

"I shouldn't think so. Even if you did get it, it might not affect you. Some people can carry it about in their body and not show any signs. That's what makes it so difficult to eradicate. And as I said, here it seems to be a range of different organisms that are causing the infections. I think that it is just coincidence that these deaths are occurring at the same time."

"Oh well. Look, I'd better be getting back. Nothing personal, but I hope I don't see you for a while."

Tom wheeled the trolley, which had been cleared by two of the other mortuary technicians, back out into the corridor and headed back to the porters rest room. The news that what had killed all these patients recently was not contagious had relieved his mind somewhat. He had been starting to have visions of himself coming down with some mysterious illness. A fit of coughing last night had worried him. His wife, Angela, had told him that it was a result of him taking smoking back up now that he had some money to spend on cigarettes again. She was probably right.

Things were going better than they had for a long time. He had the flat just how he wanted it. the car was running fine. And, most important of all, his romance with Becky was still going strong. In fact they were out virtually every night that both of them were not working. Usually it was a drive out to some quiet little pub in the country. Tonight would be different. A bouquet of flowers was waiting in the car. He showered and shaved, carefully to avoid any cuts. The last thing he wanted tonight was spots of blood on his shirt collar. He wanted to look his best. He had planned a romantic evening far out in the country, at a small family run restaurant that had been recommended to him. A quick splash with Chanel pour homme, not too much, a final comb of the hair and he was ready. It was slightly chilly outside so he decided to leave the top raised on the car. The engine caught first time and he pointed the car in the direction of Becky's house. They had been going out for only a few weeks but already he was sure. Tonight he would ask her.

Pip returned to the flat slightly the worse for wear. He had had to take a taxi, leaving the car behind at the pub. It was a great feeling to relax and let his worries fade into the distance. He had enjoyed the round of golf, and not only because he had won. The break from the pressure of work and getting away from it all with a couple of friends was just what he had needed. Poor Neil. He had to go back to the hospital - it was his night on. Tossing his jacket over a chair, Pip switched on the television and sprawled out on the couch. Within minutes he had fallen fast asleep.

Angus finally managed to leave his office at eight o'clock. It had been a long day. The only saving grace to the whole day had been when he had managed to wrap up a series of particularly nasty muggings. Most of the victims had been elderly, unable to defend themselves. The culprits, two youths of sixteen and seventeen, were in the cells. They would appear before the magistrates in the morning. He knew what he would do with them if he had his way.

He had been due at his parents house for dinner over an hour ago. Now, as he sped down the darkened road, he dialled their home number on his newly installed carphone. At the third ring the call was answered.

"Mum? It's Angus. I've not long left the office. I'll be with you in about forty minutes."

"We'll see you then dear. Drive carefully now."

"I will. 'Bye mum."

Angus broke the connection. Being an only son had its advantages, but it had its drawbacks as well. When he was younger it was the lack of a playmate when his father was tied up with the business. For all his father's absences when he was younger the two had become firm friends as Angus grew up. His mother, on the other hand, tended to fuss over him, and was continually asking him about when he was going to settle down. Not yet mother. Not while I'm having such a good time playing the field.

He drove through the double gates and proceeded up the long gravel drive to the house. About one hundred yards from the gates there was a sharp left turn which Angus delighted in taking at speed, sending up a

Dispense With Death

shower of stones. At first his mother had complained, but eventually she accepted what she called his 'childish indulgence' as the price of his weekly visit. They both knew, however, that he would still be a regular visitor even if she was the one who put her foot down about the drive.

He parked beside his mother's Mini Cooper S and his father's newly acquired Aston Martin Vanquish. A love of fast cars was a common bond between the two men and his father had promised Angus a drive in the new car tonight.

"I thought I heard you in the drive."

"Hello mum" replied Angus, giving her a quick peck on the cheek.

"I see you've been cutting the grass again", looking past him.

"What ?"

""Look at the car."

There on the Esprit's offside was the muddy evidence of Angus's misjudgement of the bend in the drive. He really would have to get back out on the track. His driving was becoming a bit sloppy.

"Sorry, I rushed it a bit because I was late. You'll still feed me, won't you?"

"Of course dear. Come on in."

The girl's fever was worsening. Neil Parsons was puzzled. despite the antibiotics, and the antipyretics, to reduce her temperature, she was steadily getting worse. perhaps a change in therapy was needed. Neil took a sample of blood and phoned the switchboard to contact the bacteriologist on call. He was surprised to find that the registrar was still in the hospital.

"Dr Warnes. Sorry to disturb you at this time of night. It's doctor Parsons here, over in Ward E. I've a patient, Catherine Smith, whom you recommended gentamicin for. There's been no improvement, in fact she's deteriorating. I've just taken a fresh blood sample. Can you check the sensitivity again?"

"You realise that it will be tomorrow now before we get any result?"

"Yes"

"Give me the lab reference number of the previous sample and I'll check it out."

Neil found the previous report in the patient's notes. He read it out over the phone.

"I'll get back to you as soon as I can."

"Okay. thanks."

Neil replaced the receiver and returned to the ward. The girl's temperature was up to 104°. The nurses had arranged two fans to play cool air around the bed.

"Nurse, do we have any ice packs?"

Dispense With Death

"There should be some in the fridge. Do you want me to get them?"

"Yes, and see if ward F have any as well. We've got to stop her temperature getting any higher."

Hermes knelt down and reached under the bed. Finding what he was looking for he slid the leather case out and laid it on top of the bed. Dialling the combinations of the lock he opened the case. He ignored the instruments, reached down and withdrew a small bottle of clear fluid. That was what he needed.

The past few weeks had given him a chance to settle into the job. The rumpus caused by those faulty trays seemed to have died down. He had had the opportunity to get to know his patients and had picked out two that would be suitable for his needs. One or two drops of the liquid that he held in his hand placed in their tea and he would be able to manipulate them as he wished. The only problem would be the presence of the nurses, but he was sure that he could find a way around that. If the worst came to the worst he had other products in his case that he could call into use.

Carefully he closed the case and locked it. He bent down and slid the deadly holdall back under the bed, pushing it as far back as possible. It was unlikely that anyone would tamper with it, but he wanted to keep it out of sight but handy should he require it. He transferred the bottle to his jacket pocket.

"Dr. Warnes? It's Neil Parsons again. That report you were going to check up on. There's no need anymore. No, the girl died fifteen minutes ago."

**Chapter 11**

Saturday morning. He had just started work. How he hated working at the weekend. Still, the extra money came in handy - it kept his car on the road and enabled him to buy those little extras that his basic salary would not stretch to.

Ben put on his white coat, switched on the tablet counter and waited for customers to come into the shop. He didn't particularly enjoy working as a locum. Even the occasional weekday locum, when the shop was busier wasn't much better, his main dislike being the moaning customers. Most of them would still be lying in their beds at this time in the morning. Having to deal with the general public was one of the reasons he had given up working as a retail pharmacist and gone to work in the hospital. It certainly wasn't the financial reward that made him do it. He had known that he was taking a drop in salary to work for the Health Service, but just how much he hadn't realised until he received his first pay slip. So, to enable him to keep on both the flat and the car, He had had to find another source of income. The easiest way was to do this, however much he disliked it. He now did a regular locum one Saturday in three, but most of the time he could see it far enough. Today was one of those days. Still, at least it was only for half the day and he would be finished at lunchtime.

He had picked Becky up early. She had a dentist's appointment and she was using the car to get there. It was a sign of their growing relationship that he had actually allowed someone else to drive his pride and joy, something he would never have envisaged happening just a few months previously.

Ten o'clock. Three hours to go. God he was bored. It was a holiday weekend and the shop was particularly quiet. All the local doctors surgeries were closed. Ben wished that the shop was too - the time was dragging so slowly. Just then he noticed old Mrs Cowan come into the shop. Instinctively he nipped into the back, out of sight. The last thing he could be bothered with today was her. Once she started talking you could never get away.

"Could I speak to the pharmacist please?"

Ben heard the words and knew that there was no way out of it. He turned to one of the shop girls.

"If I'm still with her in ten minutes, you know what to do?"

"Yes. Okay."

Fifteen minutes later the girl shouted through to him from the back shop.

"Ben, 'phone for you."

"Be right there. Sorry Mrs Cowan I'll have to go. I'll speak to you again."

"All right dear, bye bye"

"Ten minutes I told you."

"I know, but I couldn't resist it. You seemed to be enjoying yourself so much."

"Very funny. You know I don't know how she keeps going. She's always getting her tablets mixed up, or forgetting to take them. It's a shame. She's on seven different pills. No wonder she becomes confused. I would and I'm less than a third of her age."

"I think that she's lonely as well, which doesn't help. She just comes in here for a bit of company."

"I know. And the pity is that there are a lot more like her."

The hands on the clock finally managed to drag themselves around to one o'clock. Apart from the usual sprinkling of people who came looking for 'a loan of a few tablets' to see them over the holiday weekend, because they had run short, it had been yet another uneventful Saturday morning. Ben rolled his white coat into a ball and stuffed it into a plastic carrier bag. The coat could be put into the hospital laundry on Tuesday.

Becky was waiting outside for him. She had moved over into the passenger seat to let Ben drive.

"How did your appointment go?"

"Fine, no work needed - just a scale and polish. How was your morning?"

"Highly exciting" replied Ben sarcastically "let's go somewhere for the rest of the day and get away from here."

As they drove out into the country Ben thought back to the other night. Everything had been going just fine, but he hadn't had the courage to ask Becky what he had wanted to. Just relax, he had tried to tell himself and it

Dispense With Death

would be all right. But it hadn't. Maybe today it would. Ben pulled up outside a small country hotel.

"Let's have some lunch here. After that we can carry on driving and see where we end up."

Deciding to just have a pub lunch they headed for the bar. It was deserted, save for the barmaid. They ordered and sat down in an alcove. The view from the window was stunning. Less than thirty yards away the autumn sun glistened off the surface of a lake, behind which towered a range of snow capped hills. It was the perfect setting.

"Becky, will you marry me?"

***

Hermes had made a point to appear on the wards at irregular times, including the weekend. Therefore it came as no surprise to the staff nurse to see his car appear on a Saturday morning, even though it was a holiday weekend.

"Morning, staff nurse. Just thought I'd look in on Miss Talboys. How is she?"

"Her breathing is a bit difficult. I think that she may have some catarrh in her throat that she can't clear. Apart from that she's no different."

"I'll go and have a look at her."

Miss Talboys had a room to herself - a rare luxury in the psychogeriatric unit. Most of the other patients spent their lives in a communal ward, with only a single wardrobe and a bedside locker in which to keep all of their possessions. Some of the patients had lived in the ward for over twenty years, if lived was the right word to describe their pathetic existence. The nurses did their best for the patients, but medically they had been left behind. When Hermes first arrived he found medicine Kardexes that had been written over twenty years ago and that were still in current use. One of his first tasks had been to revise and update most of the patient's medication. The results had been remarkable - one or two of the patients had improved to such a degree that they had gone home to their families this weekend as a trial to test how they would cope outside the hospital, with a view to their eventually being discharged from the hospital.

Hermes entered Miss Talboys's room and sat down on the edge of her bed.
"How are you today. I hear that your breathing is giving you a bit of difficulty.

Don't worry, we'll soon get that sorted out. I'm just going to give you a couple of injections to help you. I'll be back in a minute."

Hermes removed the necessary drugs from the cupboard and prepared a tray for them with two syringes and some swabs. He went back into the room and drew the curtain around the bed to block the view to the bed.

There was no response as he tightened the tourniquet around the woman's arm. He prepared the syringe containing the analgesia and laid it to one side. Then he withdrew a vial from his jacket pocket and transferred its contents into the second syringe. Taking care not to miss the vein he slowly emptied the contents of the syringe into the woman's arm. He released the

Dispense With Death

tourniquet and within seconds he saw the pain in her eyes. It had not taken as long as he had expected. He quickly picked the other syringe from the tray and injected the painkiller into the arm. It was a high enough dose to relieve the pain that he had just inflicted and to induce drowsiness. He waited for a few minutes until Miss Talboys was sleeping peacefully.

"She's fine now nurse" said Hermes as he dropped the syringes into a sharps disposal bin. "She's sleeping. Keep an eye on her for me, will you. I'll just look in on another couple of patients on my way out."

As he drove Hermes reflected on the morning's work. The speed of the old woman's reaction to the chemical had taken him by surprise. He would have to revise what he had planned. Still it was a beginning. It was a true saying - the eyes are the window of the soul. They had been the ideal way to measure the woman's pain response. She hadn't uttered a sound in years - it was a part of her condition. It was unlikely that she would remember what had happened and if she did - well he had given the analgesic virtually instantaneously and any recollection of pain that she had would be put down the confusion due to a combination of her condition and the analgesic. The call that he had paid on the other two patients had merely been routine to act as a cover for the visit to Miss Talboys in case anything had gone wrong. Yes, things were going very nicely. Next week he would start in earnest.

The Saturday afternoon and evening shift in casualty was not one that he enjoyed. However, along with the other SHO's he had to take his turn. The afternoon wasn't so bad. It was night-time, especially the period just after the pubs closed. That was when things started to get busy - gang fights, car crashes, broken limbs.

And nearly all the admissions caused by alcohol. Mind you, he was one to talk. How he had made it home after the golf match he still didn't know. He did remember that Pip had won the match and that they had gone to the pub afterwards. The next he remembered was waking up with a thumping headache and a decidedly dodgy stomach. Not for the first time did he promise himself to stop drinking. And no doubt it wouldn't be the last time that he made the promise.

Nothing much happened for the first few hours - a few cuts and sprains, the occasional child who had fallen and banged their head. Nothing major. Then, just after three o'clock an ambulance came screeching in, lights flashing. The crew had radioed in with details so Bill was prepared. A young woman of 23 from the local council housing estate. She had taken a mixture of pills and washed them down with what was thought to be a bottle of gin. A neighbour had called on her to go shopping and getting no answer to the door bell had let herself in to find her friend slumped in a chair, the empty tablet bottles on a table beside her.

The ambulance crew wheeled her into the nearest treatment room. She was lapsing in and out of consciousness. Two nurses held her still while Bill pumped her stomach. It hadn't been too long since she had taken the overdose because he could clearly identify the remains of some of the drugs. That was a good sign - there was a good chance that most of the drugs had not yet been absorbed into her system. A few hours sleeping it off in a ward and then a visit from a psychiatrist should sort her out.

Just then the sister burst into the cubicle

Dispense With Death

"RTA. Car and a bicycle. Should be here in ten minutes."

Five minutes later two ambulances drew up at the door, followed by a police car. Bill knew straight away that the occupant of the first ambulance was dead.

"He was on the bike. Never stood a chance" said one of the ambulancemen, as he wheeled the body through the reception area.

"Wheel him over there, will you. We'll deal with him later. Let's concentrate on the living just now."

The second ambulance contained a young couple. The girl had a nasty gash on her head. She would need an x-ray, just in case of any non-visible damage. The other occupant was a boy who couldn't have been more than eighteen, looking very anxious. He was followed in by two policemen.

Bill attended to the girl. She had a bruise on her forehead and the cut needed a couple of stitches. The x-ray showed no other damage but he decided to keep her in overnight for observation. It wasn't till later when the staff had a chance to grab a cup of coffee that he heard what had happened.

"The man was on his bicycle and cycled straight out of a side street into the path of the car. The young boy never had a hope of avoiding him."

"Had he been drinking?"

"The boy - no. Neither had the man. He just hadn't looked where he was going. The girl wasn't wearing a seatbelt and hit the windscreen. She was lucky not to go

Dispense With Death 84

through it. It's the boy that I feel sorry for. He was worried about his girlfriend, it was his dad's car and he was really upset about the man. We calmed him down as best we could and the police took him home."

"Poor kid. I hope we don't get any more like that tonight."


"Can I have the news desk please?"

"One moment"

It was one o'clock. The silence was suddenly interrupted by the ringing of the telephone. Probably just another mugging or gang fight, thought the reporter as he picked up the receiver.

"News desk"

"I've got something that might interest you."

"Oh yes. What might that be?"
"There's something funny going on over at the hospital."

"What do you mean - something funny?"

"There have been a few deaths over the past week or so that have the doctors baffled."

"People do die in hospital and often it is very difficult to pinpoint the exact cause" The reporter was tempted to hang up, classing it as another drunk having a laugh. He decided to give it another minute or so.

"Yes, but six people in three days, in the same block of wards."

The reporter sensed the beginnings of a good story. Things had been quiet lately and a good story would liven things up.

"Can you back this up?"

"Well the patient records would give you a good start."

"If we send someone round tomorrow would you be willing to talk?"

There was no reply. The caller had hung up. Was it a crank? There was only one way to find out. He made a note in the diary to call round on Monday.


One o'clock in the morning and the department was quiet. Only three drunks and a knife wound - it must have been a record for a Saturday night. From now on in the shift was easy going. Bill looked forward to 8 o'clock when he would be finished.

Ben lay on top of the bed, staring at the ceiling. It was three in the morning. He was still wide awake after the day's happenings - a day which he reflected was the happiest of his life. Becky had not been expecting his question.

"Will you marry me?"

"What?"

"Will you marry me?"

"Gosh, I don't know what to say. You've sprung this on me."

"Just say yes."

"Yes."

"You mean it?"

"Yes. Yes I do. These past few weeks have been wonderful. What will my parents say? We've only been going out for a few weeks. They'll have a fit."

"Don't tell them. Not just yet. Let's wait until Christmas and announce it then. That way it won't seem so sudden to them. That'll also give us time to choose the ring. In fact why don't we go back into town and look in a few jewellers."

They then spent the rest of the afternoon looking around the local jewellers. Becky had spotted a couple of rings that she quite liked, fortunately in the price range that Ben could afford. They arranged to meet later on to go out for a celebration meal. After dropping Becky off at her home Ben had returned to the shops and bought a huge bouquet of flowers and the biggest box of chocolates that he could find.

Becky had opened the door to find Ben standing there, immaculately dressed, with both hands behind his back. Before she could say anything both hands appeared, the chocolates in one, the flowers in the other.

"They're gorgeous. You shouldn't have bought so much though. They must have cost a fortune."

"You're worth it."

Ben had booked a table at the restaurant in the local hotel. The meal had been average, the prices above it. He hadn't cared. It had been a wonderful night. He hadn't wanted to leave Becky but knew that he had to. They had an understanding, an unspoken rule, no sex. That they would keep for their married life. So, reluctantly, Ben had taken her home. Becky had invited him in for coffee. Both her parents were in bed. They had sat kissing and cuddling on the sofa. The coffee went cold, undrunk. Finally Ben felt that he should leave, whilst it was still a decent hour.

He decided that he should really get ready for bed. That way he might eventually fall asleep. An old school friend was coming round to the flat in the morning, and then they were going out for a game of squash.

At about 4 o'clock Ben eventually drifted off to sleep, a smile still etched on his face. Just about the same time a cigarette in a flat further up the street smouldered away, unnoticed down the back of an armchair. Within half an hour the chair was ablaze, filling the room with choking black smoke. Bill's quiet night was about to be interrupted.

## Chapter 12

The last thing that Donald Layne needed was the banner headline in tonight's local paper :-

# POLICE INVESTIGATE SUSPICIOUS DEATHS IN LOCAL HOSPITAL

As Hospital General Manager he would be the one who would have to sort out the problems that would result.

That morning a reporter from the paper had come to see him. The day after a public holiday was busy enough without having to deal with the press but, reluctantly, Donald had agreed to see him. He thought that they had come to an agreement to keep the story quiet for the moment.

"Mr Layne? John Dorsey, from The News. I'm following up a call that we received over the weekend."

"Uh huh, and what has that to do with me?"

"It concerns this hospital." Dorsey recounted the story that had been phoned into the paper. As he did so Donald's face became more serious as he considered the implications.

"And he didn't leave his name?"

"No."

"Or say that he worked here?"

"No, he just rang off."

"Well to be totally honest with you I would be tempted to put it down as a crank call. I've heard nothing about a series of suspicious deaths. Look, can I call you this afternoon, after I've had a chance to check it out. However I think that you will find that there is nothing in it."

"Fine, I'll do nothing about it until then."

As Dorsey left the office a secretary entered followed by Angus Critchley.

"D.I. Critchley. What brings you here?"

"Nothing that would interest you. Just leaving?"

"Yes" Dorsey turned back to Layne. "Until this afternoon"

Once out of the office Dorsey held back to try and catch the conversation between Angus and the manager.

"We received a call early this morning. Anonymous. Alleging a series of suspicious deaths. Now as we know this is the second time in the past few weeks that we've been "

"Right you, get out."

Dorsey was hauled away by a young man who had just come into the outer office.

"It's all right. I'm just going. I've heard enough."

The mistake that Donald had made was not to call the reporter back. He had been preoccupied with other matters and pushed it to the back of his mind. Now he was about to pay for it.

"Miss Richard, get me Mr Dorsey at the local paper, would you please?"

Donald threw the paper down in disgust. Flimsy information, based on a phone call, had been plastered all over the front page as fact.

"Mr Dorsey. What's the meaning of this story. We agreed that you would go no further until you heard from me."

"Not quite. You should have called me back. Anyway the situation altered. Can you deny that the police are carrying out an investigation in the hospital."

"No"

"Or that this is the second time recently that they've done so?"

"No, but that was on an unrelated matter. Nothing at all to do with the 'suspicious deaths' that you talk about."

"Nevertheless the basis of the story is true. You just confirmed it."

"Yes, but if you had allowed me to finish you would have heard the full story, instead of just barging in. Yes, the police did carry out an investigation recently. In fact they arrived just as you were leaving this

morning. Hold on a minute - you must have been listening in. That's how you knew, wasn't it?"
"You know that I can't reveal my sources. Anyway you were saying."

The despicable little man. Layne hated any underhand dealings. He believed in being straightforward with people. People like Dorsey annoyed him intensely. His immediate reaction was to slam the phone down, but that would be counter productive.

"The police received the same call that you did. Anonymous, but they had to follow it up anyway. I was being truthful when I told you this morning that I knew nothing about any suspicious deaths. All that your caller's 'suspicious deaths' amounted to were some deaths in the surgical unit in a relatively short space of time and we thought that there might be a connection between them. But there was none whatsoever. It was just one of those things that happen in a large hospital. Sick people die. Sometimes more die than normal. The police are satisfied that there's nothing in it. You jumped the gun for a bit of sensationalism."

"I wouldn't say that. Only doing our public duty."

"And is your public duty to terrify the local population, such that they don't want to come to their local hospital because they might not come back out? Your story could end up killing more people than the number in your article. How about waiting for all the facts the next time instead of making up a story based on what you hear through keyholes. I hope that there will be a retraction in tomorrow's edition."

"Not a retraction. What we printed today was true. We'll just finish the story off tomorrow."

"Yes, no doubt buried well inside the paper."

Layne slammed the phone down. It was always the same. Splash bad news all over the front page. Good news, or a follow up to a 'scoop' that is not tasty enough to sell papers, can be hidden somewhere in the inner pages.

***

Hermes's initial pleasure at Miss Talboys reaction to the drugs had soon subsided when he realised that he was going to be restricted by the confines of the ward system. If he routinely appeared in the ward at unusual hours he would soon draw attention to himself. Normally any other consultant would not mind this but a low profile was something Hermes was determined to keep. Today he had returned to the ward to look in on another patient, this time an elderly Italian gentleman Mr Fiorio.

The man had been resident in the ward for fifteen years and there was no possibility of him ever leaving, except in a box. He had come to Britain in the early 1930's and set himself up in business running a small corner shop. On the outbreak of war he, along with many of his fellow countrymen, had been rounded up and interned for the duration. When he was released he had started from scratch and built the business back up.

Unfortunately his experience during the war had affected him more than was at first apparent and gradually his mental function began to deteriorate, eventually culminating in his hospitalisation. He was now in an advanced state of senility and was barely lucid. Today he had been particularly distressed - it was the anniversary of his internment and no matter how poor his mental function at other times, this date appeared burned indelibly into his subconscious.

"I'll take these in with me" said Hermes, picking up the tranquillisers that the staff nurse had prepared.

"He's due his monthly depot injection as well" said the nurse. "Do you want to do that at the same time?"

"Why not".

Hermes waited until the nurse brought the new vial from the drug cupboard. What he didn't want was to start his treatment and the nurse to come in halfway through.

The nurse made to follow him into Fiorio's room.

"It's all right" said Hermes "I'll manage. It might be better for just one of us to go in anyway. Less frightening for him in his present state."

Hermes now had the room to himself. He repeated the procedure that he had used on Miss Talboys, but this time there was absolutely no response. The man was so far gone that even the extreme pain that Hermes had just inflicted had had no apparent effect. Hermes drew up Fiorio's dose from the vial of depot injection and administered the drug. he was about to throw the remains of the vial away when a thought came to him. There was a way he could overcome having to use the patients in the ward all the time. Hermes placed the vial in his pocket and discarded the used syringes.

When he got back to the flat Hermes divided the remains of the vial into three containers. From his case he removed three vials of clear liquid. He added a small amount of each to each container of the drug. The first solution curdled. The second stayed in two distinct layers. When he added the third solution to the drug the two solutions mixed perfectly.

The depot injection that Hermes had pocketed was a special formulation of drug commonly used in the wards. The drug was specially prepared in an oily solution so that when it was injected into a patient's muscle the drug was only released slowly. In that way patients who were unlikely to take their medication regularly could be treated with a monthly injection at the out patients clinic.

If Hermes could add some of his chosen drug to the vials to be used at a clinic session he could treat a few patients in one go and reassess the effect in one months time.

**Chapter 13**

Hermes had soon grown bored with experimenting on the elderly patients. Their lack of reaction dismayed him. The effects of the drug over a month had been minimal. he had increased the dosage as much as he dared without it becoming obvious that he had tampered with the vials in the clinic. So far no-one had died as a result of his doings but he accepted that it was only a question of time. That could prove uncomfortable. He decided that he really needed people of a younger age group.

The ideal subjects would be the nurses in the ward. They were accessible, and being younger would be able to withstand his experimentation better. He would have to manipulate them until they were suitably disposed for his needs. There was one particular student that he had already picked out as a suitable candidate.

He returned to the flat to work out a strategy. For that he needed his cases. These were now secreted within a partitioning wall that had been built as part of general works that he had had carried out. Once the workmen had finished Hermes had made some more alterations of his own. The panels were virtually undetectable, but enabled quick and easy access when necessary.

Hermes removed the panel and took out the case which contained his equipment. Unlocking it he removed the upper compartment. It was just as he thought. He had miscalculated his heroin requirements. The past few weeks had used up most of his stock. Obtaining more would be a problem. There was no way he could use any of the stock from the wards. It was too tightly controlled and the quantity that he needed would be missed immediately. There was only one thing for it. He would have to obtain supplies 'on the street'. It would be tricky but he was sure that by using suitable tactics he would be able to work his way up the drugs pipeline far enough to enable him to obtain heroin of a reasonable quality.

He quickly changed out of the suit into a pair of black cords and a black crew neck sweater. A pair of dark training shoes and a dark windcheater completed the outfit. From the bottom of the case he removed two small objects which he placed in the jacket pocket. Two hundred pounds from his wallet and his keys. Now he was ready. No identification.

Hermes knew exactly where to go for heroin. Working in the psychiatric unit had brought him into occasional contact with drug addicts. Through them he had discovered where to obtain supplies. The drug abuse problem was widespread and growing. It would take him only 45 minutes in the car to be far enough away that no-one would know him, but still be able to obtain heroin.
He found a pusher easily enough, they were on virtually every street corner. It did not take him long to get past this stage of the chain and find out where to go next. This took him to a very rundown area of the town. Still, he had been in worse areas back home, but, nevertheless, he would have to watch his step. Following the directions that he had been given he turned into an alleyway, all his senses alert. The buildings rose on either side, blocking out all the light. The far end of the alleyway glowed eerily in the distance. Hermes slowed and allowed his eyes to adjust to the gloom. He removed one of the two objects from his pocket and continued cautiously down the alley. He had gone about halfway when he became aware of

someone just behind him. He dived to his left just as a length of pipe crashed into the wall at the level where his chest had been moments earlier. Hermes switched on the small torch that he held in his hand. The torch gave out a light belying its size, blinding the assailant momentarily.

Springing up quickly Hermes grabbed the pipe, twisting it downwards and prizing it from the man's grip. Seconds later the attacker was powerless, Hermes right knee pressing into his lower back, the pipe pulled tight across his throat.

"I'm going to move the pipe slightly. But the slightest movement from you and I'll increase the force on your throat. Understand?"

The man nodded his head, slightly.

"Good" said Hermes, as he lessened his grip on the pipe. "Now, who are you?"

"Go fuck yourself."

Hermes reapplied the pressure on the man's neck, only this time using more force.

"Any more of that and this pipe will break your neck. Now who are you?"

"You wanted to meet me."

"And do you always greet your visitors in such a friendly manner?"

"I don't like people harassing my dealers. It makes them nervous. We have enough trouble with the police without newcomers muscling in on the territory. What is it that you want?"

"First, tell your pal back there not to try anything if you want to remain able to walk."

"Stay where you are Dave. Don't do anything."

"Now, lets do business. How much do you charge?"

"You want to buy. You don't look like a dealer. Why do you want it?"

"Never mind. How much?"

"Ten pounds a packet. You can cut that into four and sell at five each."

"Two fifty."

"What! It costs me four. Five pounds. I can't go lower than that."

"How pure is it?"

"Twenty per cent"

Hermes increased the pressure on the man's neck.

"All right. Fifteen per cent. I cut it further before the dealers get it for the streets, but you can have it as I get it."

"How much have you got?"

"20 grams"

"I'm going to let you go now. But don't get any ideas about trying anything OK?"

Hermes released the man and shifted his position to enable him to keep both men in his sights. Taking the notes from his pocket he counted out the money required. When he agreed on a price he stuck to it. He could have the heroin for nothing but it wasn't in his nature to do business like that. Besides if the drug was good enough he would come back for more. He quickly tested the powder that the man gave him and handed over the cash.

"It's all there. If I need more I know where to find you. Now beat it."

An hour later Hermes was back in the flat. It was just after 11 o'clock and the night's action had given him a boost. Now he couldn't wait to get started again. He changed out of the black clothes and back into a suit.

The student nurse was slightly taken aback to find Dr Hermes in the ward on a Sunday night. That he was sitting in the duty room having made coffee for both of them surprised her even more.

"You looked as though you could do with a cup of coffee. Sit down. Milk and sugar?"

"Yes please. Two spoonfuls. You're not normally in on a Sunday night are you?"

"I was doing some paperwork and thought that I would have a look in. How do you like having to work on a Sunday night?" Wouldn't you rather be out at a disco or something?"

Dispense With Death

"It's not too bad once you get used to it. I've had to work a double shift. Still it'll be worth it when I get my pay."

"This is a special blend that I've had sent over from Spain. Try it out, I think you'll like it."

Hermes removed a small packet from his pocket and tipped 10mg of heroin into the cup of coffee. It dissolved instantly. Taking care not to mix the cups up he returned to the table. "It's quite bitter" said Becky.

"Yes, but only at first. Don't be put off by your first taste. At least try the whole cup."

Fifteen minutes later and Becky had finished the whole drink. There was a look of contentment on her face. That was very nice. Where did you say that you got it from.?"

"It's Spanish. I've only a small supply."

"That's a pity. It was really nice. I wish I hadn't sat down. I feel really tired."

Yes, you would thought Hermes. In addition to the heroin there was enough chloral hydrate in the cup to make her feel drowsy, but not enough to knock her out. Over the next few weeks he would gradually up the dose and possibly add in some other drugs. Eventually she would be ready for something special that he wanted to try out. He had a supply of ricin with him. This was a highly toxic poison which only required a very small quantity to be fatal. The most famous example of it's use was the murder of Bulgarian Georgi Markov in London, in the 1970's, when he had been injected with the poison via an umbrella tip. Hermes had managed to prepare a very weak solution for injection that he wanted to try out to observe the side effects.

## Chapter 14

"How would you like to come to my house for your Christmas dinner?" had been the invitation from Becky and Ben had jumped at the offer. The hours that he was working over the holiday period meant that he wasn't going to make it to his parent's home this year and all that he had to look forward to was Christmas dinner alone in the flat.

"Wont all your family be there?"

"Just my mum and dad, and my younger brother."

"OK. I'd be spending it alone in the flat otherwise."

Now that the holiday season was approaching he had noticed that Becky seemed to be almost permanently tired, but he put it down to the extra hours that she was working. They hadn't been able to go out together much, and the plans for the wedding had taken a back seat. One night, while she was on duty, Ben had gone down to the pub with Tom.

"Becky's looking very tired lately."

"Yes. her mum and me have been trying to tell her not to work so much overtime, but she wont listen. Every penny is being saved for the wedding."

"I know. I've cut back drastically this year on presents. People will just have to understand that I have other things to do with my money."

"She's been getting cheeky recently as well. And that's not like her."

"Nothing to do with me. I've hardly seen her over the past two weeks, what with her working all the time."

"Maybe once this busy spell is over she'll be back to her usual self."


Drugs were something Angus despised. he sometimes felt sorry for the addicts, but a lot of them only had themselves to blame. It was the dealers that he reserved most of his anger for. These peddlers of death really made him see red. They didn't give a damn how many young lives they ruined - all they were interested in was maximising their profit. He had known some of them to give the heroin away at first, then when the kid was hooked, move in hard and they had another regular customer.

He had been on the current case for two weeks. One or two of the dealers had been picked up, but these had mainly been dealing to finance their own habit. They had been released on bail almost immediately. It was those further up the chain that the police were after - the Mister Bigs who sat back and raked in thousands of pounds in profits.

As seemed to be the case all over the country the dealers were to be found in the more squalid areas of the cities. There you could see the younger children behind the tenements with crisp bags over their mouths - solvent sniffing. Unless the dealers were stamped out soon those children would graduate onto hard drugs - just like their older brothers and sisters.

The Lotus was parked in the police garage. After all, it did not exactly look right in this area. Instead an old beaten up Ford escort was pressed into service. As well as the car Angus had to forego his usual sartorial elegance and instead dress in the scruffiest clothes that could be found. D.C. Coll was similarly attired. Through word of mouth they had eventually been added to a dealer's list of clients. The first deal had been concluded without any hitches. When they returned the following day the flat was raided. Angus and Norman had been taken into custody, to give the impression that the bust had not been a set-up. Later on that day the routine was repeated, but on the opposite side of town. That had left the police with two small time dealers in custody. Angus was to interview one of them, Norman the other.

"Now then Harry" said Angus, as he closed the cell door behind him "you've got yourself into a nice tight little corner, haven't you?"

Harry jumped up from the chair. "You bastard. It was all a set-up. I should have known."

"A bit careless of you. Still we all make mistakes, don't we."

"I only sell the stuff to get money for my own habit. I don't make any money out of it."

"'Course you don't. You give it away don't you. Nice jacket. Leather, isn't it? Bet that cost a pretty penny."

"I'm saying no more till I see my lawyer."

"Come on Harry. We both know you're for the high jump. It just a question of how long you get. I'm sure that you understand. We don't want small fry like you. I'll see you later."

Dispense With Death

Angus got up and left the cell. Norman was waiting outside in the corridor.

"How did you get on?"

"Bit of a dead end. Our friend claims to get his supplies from Harry in there. I think that he's genuine. There's no way that he can know that we've picked up Harry."

"True. Still it does mean that Harry is higher up than he's been letting on. If he knows that we know that it might make him more willing to co-operate."

"Well now Harry, we haven't been telling the nice policeman the truth, have we?"

"Course I have."

"I don't think so. You see we know that you supply to other dealers. In fact we've got one of them down the corridor. Told us that he gets his stuff from you. Now that means that you are looking at ten years at least, maybe fifteen. If you help us we might be able to cut it a bit."

The look of defeat on Harry's face told Angus that he had won. Now it was just a question of working out the details.

"Where do you get your heroin - London?"

"No I'm not that well connected. I get it from just outside town."

"Come on Harry, if you want our help you'll have to do better than that."

Forty five minutes later Angus left the cell armed with all the information he needed. Now for the next stage.

Hermes was in a foul mood. He should have known better than to trust a common criminal. The heroin he had bought wasn't of the quality that he had expected. In fact, it was only about 10% pure. At that potency his supply would be quickly exhausted. If he was to continue his work he needed better quality. He would have to pay the dealer another visit, only this time he would choose the time and place, and the dealer wouldn't know about it in advance. This time he wouldn't be looking for drugs but a name. The further up he managed to work himself the better quality drug that he could obtain, and therefore the less often he would have to expose himself to the risk of being caught. It dismayed him to have to associate with, and be dependant on, such people but he had no choice in his present situation.

Dressing quickly he checked that he had everything that he required. Taking the thin wire garrotte was a calculated risk. There was no easy way to explain away its presence if he was caught. Still he did not intend to get caught. With any luck he would not have to use it. The last thing that he wanted was the police snooping around the drug scene investigating a gruesome murder. He slipped it into his inside pocket. in the same pocket he added a small pre-filled syringe. Taking care to set all the alarms Hermes locked up the flat and headed for the lift.

After about an hours drive he parked the car. The final part of the journey would have to be made on foot. The car was distinctive and he did not want anyone to spot it. The streets were quiet, not many people about. It had started to get frosty even though it was only 8 o'clock. Within ten minutes Hermes had the dealer's flat almost in sight. As he rounded the corner he froze, the sight greeting him putting him on full alert.

Angus was all set to go. The flat had been under surveillance by the local beat bobbies. They had reported one or two visitors, but these had been allowed to go their way. Nothing was to be done to arouse the suspicions of the man who lived in the flat. Too much was at stake to balls things up now. Angus and Norman were to go in first with backup teams following them. All possible exits from the flat had been covered.

Angus walked into the close, followed by Norman. All the other officers were out of sight. If the dealer caught sight of any unusual activity all the evidence would go down the toilet pan, taking the police case with it. As they reached the door Angus removed the two-way radio from his pocket.
"We're going in now. Everybody move in."
There was no time for niceties. A sledgehammer followed by a well placed size 9 boot made short work of the door. Norman caught a glimpse of the dealer closing the toilet door. He put his shoulder to the door. No joy. the boot was brought back into play and the door gave way.

"no you don't" said Norman as he stopped the dealer from flushing the toilet. As he forced the man away from the toilet Angus leaned down and retrieved the small polythene bags from the bowl and place them in an evidence bag.

"He's all yours. take him away." called Norman to the two officers just coming through the front door.

Dispense With Death

"And take good care of this" said Angus as he handed over the plastic bag "We'll take a look around and speak to him later."

The flat was tawdry and cheap. Most probably used as a dealing point and no more. The lack of heavies, or strengthening of the door puzzled him. Either the dealer was crazy and thought he could get away with the economies, or the heavies were around somewhere. If that was the case they would not go far. There were enough police officers around to make sure of that.

"Let's get out of this dump. We'll leave it to the local boys to clear up here. I wonder how much we'll get out of him. I'd hate to have gone through all this for one lousy dealer."

As they left the close Angus noticed a man on the other side of the street. The man stood for a second and then walked quickly away when he noticed Angus looking at him. It crossed Angus's mind that it could be one of the missing minders. As he made to follow the man Norman came up to him.

"We've got the minder. He tried to sneak out the back but two of the boys caught him."

"What do you make of him over there?" said Angus, but when he turned around the man was nowhere to be seen.

"Who?"

"Oh, it's probably nothing. Probably a junkie, and we scared him off."

Dispense With Death

There was something about the man. He did not look like the average junkie. Angus put it out of his mind. Possibly just a passer-by who didn't want to become involved when he saw all the police activity. Anyway it had been a reasonable night. He was off home.

As soon as he was out of sight Hermes broke into a jog. All those police! If he had been five minutes earlier he would have been caught. And one of the police had seen him - he was sure of that. He looked back. No-one was following him. He reached the car and sat inside to get his breath back. Dealing with the drugs trade was too dangerous. If he had been caught... The thought didn't bear thinking about. He would just have to make the supplies he had last until he came up with a less dangerous alternative. He started the car.

As he drove along the country roads Hermes made up his mind. Much as it disappointed him to do so, he would have to give up on his experimentation, at least for the time being. Tonight had finally settled it. For the past few days he had been thinking it over. The adverse publicity about the hospital in the local paper had started it off. Although they had printed what amounted to a retraction of the original story the hospital was still high on people's minds. He hadn't known about the two police investigations. And the nurse he was using was friendly with one of the pharmacists. If he had been caught tonight that would have been it. Good as his cover story was, if the police started digging into it they would eventually find out the truth. No. He would lay off for a while. Hopefully the police officer hadn't recognised him.

He drove into the underground car park and parked the BMW in his reserved space. Setting the alarm he then took the lift up to his flat. Only when he was safely inside did he remove the garrotte from his pocket. Taking the cases from their hiding place he replaced the equipment and reset the locks. They would be safe until he required them again. How long that would be was anyone's guess - weeks, months. It would soon be Christmas - that would become the focus of peoples attention. Not him though. The season of goodwill was not his favourite time of year. The fact that he was alone in Britain did not bother him unduly. For him the holiday season was just a two week disruption. Stripping off he extinguished the room light. Within five minutes he was fast asleep.

Pip had been doing a lot of thinking over the past few weeks. Although no-one actually said as much he could feel the shadow of the trays looming over him. Maybe he was becoming paranoid about the incident. No other cause had been found and Pip felt that he had been found guilty by default. He felt that the consultants attitude to him had changed, although it may have been more down to his imagination than anything else. And it wasn't just the consultants, even the attitude of nursing staff towards him seemed to have changed. But he hadn't done anything wrong, that was the galling thing. Admittedly he had sometimes doubted himself, but when he thought it out he always came back to the same answer. Everything he had done was right. He couldn't have done any more if he had tried.

He had gradually come to realise that, unless the situation was cleared up to his satisfaction, he would never get any further on in the hospital. With that in mind he had applied for several vacancies that were being advertised, just to get away and start afresh somewhere else. With so many doctors unemployed he had been lucky to get a job with only his third application. It would mean a months gap between jobs but that couldn't be helped.

Selling the flat hadn't been as easy. The shifts he worked made it difficult to show prospective purchasers around. It was with reluctance that he put the flat on the books of a local estate agent. At least they would have to work for their money. After a few weeks a young couple put in an offer. It was lower than he really wanted but, reluctantly, Pip accepted it. They had been the only people to have shown any interest, and he wanted to have the flat sold before Christmas.

The hospital administrator hadn't been too pleased when Pip told him that he would be leaving after New Year, but Pip no longer cared. As far as he was concerned the hospital could get stuffed.

Now Christmas time was approaching and although he would be on duty on Christmas day he was quite looking forward to it. All the patients that were able would be discharged home to spend the holiday season with their families. This left only a few patients in the hospital to be looked after. As a result the staff managed to create a party atmosphere in the hospital.

He had taken a weeks holiday which had been badly needed. A few days in France sampling the local produce had been just what he had needed. But, all too soon it was over and he returned to work. Now, although it was just two weeks previous, the holiday was but a distant memory. Never mind. Only two more patient discharge prescriptions to write out and he was off duty for two days. And then there came that familiar, unwelcome, sound as the bleep was going off yet again. What now?

Pip picked up the nearest telephone and called the ward. A few minutes later he hung up. It looked as if he would be working for some time yet.

**Chapter 15**

Christmas Eve. Outside the snow was falling heavily. At that moment Ben wasn't interested in the fact that Christmas would be white. All that bothered him was when he would get home.

Somehow he had ended up doing a locum today. Still, the money would come in handy for their savings. The shop was full of customers buying last minute presents. It was always the same.

"Prescription for you, Mr Brosan."

Ben lifted his head from the journal he had been reading and took the prescription from the counter assistant. He was just about to count out the tablets when something made him look again. Why he did so he wasn't sure, but there was something odd about the writing that he wasn't happy about, especially as the script was for a drug that he knew was abused locally by addicts. The boy who handed in the script was sitting in the waiting area. He looked respectable enough - smartly groomed and tidily dressed - although that counted for nothing these days. A quick check showed that the pad was not on the list of those stolen. The list, however, was always a week or two out of date because of the time lag between the doctor notifying the script's loss and the letter coming out to the local pharmacies. Ben decided to contact the doctor and punched out the number on the phone. As he expected there was no answer and after ten rings there was a click as the surgery answering machine tripped into life. When the deputising number had been spoken Ben put the receiver down, keyed in the new number and waited. After what seemed an age the phone was answered.

"Hello, this is Baker's Pharmacy. I have a script that I would like to confirm with Doctor Oldfield."

"I'll try and contact him. Can you give me your number and I'll have him call you."

Ben recited the shop number and put the phone down. The boy had disappeared from the shop. That confirmed Ben's suspicion. The delay in the dispensing of the script had panicked him and he was gone.

Ten minutes later Dr Oldfield returned Ben's call and confirmed that he had not written the script. Ben dialled the local police station. It wasn't long before two uniformed officers came into the shop. Ben had told the desk sergeant that there was no point in rushing as the lad had gone, but the police had been in the area anyway.

"We'll take this as evidence" said one of the constables, picking up the prescription by its corner. "From your description I've a good idea who the lad was. You'd recognise him if you saw him again?"

"Yes."

"Would you mind coming to the station once you've finished here. I know it's Christmas Eve, but it might help to get this finished with."

"All right. I finish at one o'clock. I'll come down then."

"Ask at the desk for the CID and explain why you're there.

Dispense With Death

It was nearly half past one by the time Ben had tidied up and driven to the police station. He sat down while he waited for a detective to take him to a room to look at some mugshots.

When the detective arrived Ben recognised him as one of those who had been at the hospital pharmacy recently.

"Hello. I'm Detective Constable Coll. Glad you could spare the time to come down."

"Yes. We've met before. In the hospital pharmacy a few weeks ago."

"Oh yes, I remember. Unfortunate business that. Now you're here to look at a few photos, is that right?"

"Yes. I received a forged prescription this afternoon and two of your uniformed colleagues took it away. The guy who handed it in got away, but I think that I would possibly recognise him if I saw him again."

"There's three books of photos over here. Just work your way through them. Some are a bit out of date I'm afraid. I'll pop in and out to see how you're getting on."

Two hours later Ben turned over the last page. It had been a waste of time. The face was nowhere to be seen in any of the books.

"I'm sorry. I don't see him here at all."

"Not to worry. The description that you gave us was quite good. There are a couple of groups of drug addicts around the area. We'll keep a look out for him amongst them. Thanks for all your help, coming in today of all days."

"That's all right. I always like to help. The more of these junkies we catch the easier it will be for all of us."

"Yes. You'll hear if we get him. You may have to give evidence if there's a trial. Anyway, hope it hasn't spoiled you Christmas."

Ben left the building and ran to his car. 4 o'clock and he still had more presents to buy for Becky. At least the shops would be opened late. Oh well, better go and brave the last minute rush.


Christmas Day. For the first time in years it was a white one. The overnight fall of snow had crisped up on top and Tom and Ben crunched down the street on their way to the local pub for a pre-dinner drink.

"Best to get out of the women's way for a while. I've always found that the thing to do. Linda's always telling me that I just get under her feet."

"Good excuse to get out for a quick drink"

"Gives us a chance for a little chat."

"Oh"

"About Becky. Have you noticed anything recently?"

"In what way?"

"Are you two all right. I mean there's nothing wrong is there?"

Dispense With Death

"Not that I know. There would have been if I hadn't managed to buy her present last night. though. In fact we intend to start house hunting in the New Year."

"I thought that you would just stay in the flat."

"No. It's not really big enough. It looks like we'll try to buy a house, complete with garden."

"You don't seem too pleased about that."

"It's just that I've never done any gardening before."

"Don't worry about that. I'll help you get started."

The pub was almost deserted. The barmaid looked bored. No doubt she would have preferred to be at home with her family. Still, someone had to serve the customers. Tom ordered two pints and sat down at one of the tables. After a few minutes Ben brought the subject of Becky back up.

"What makes you think that something is wrong?" asked Ben.

"It's just over the past few weeks "said Tom, handing Ben his pint of beer "She seems to get a bit irritable when she comes home from work."

"Well she has got exams coming up. I suppose that, coupled with the wedding preparations, might be getting to her."

"Have you two set a date yet?"

"Not exactly. We were thinking about late August, but haven't decided for definite yet."

"You had better get a move on otherwise every place will be fully booked."

"I know. Do you think that we should head back now?"

Tom looked at the clock behind the bar. "No, give it another twenty minutes. We'll only be told that we're in the way if we go back now. Anyway, its your round."

"In that case, do you want another?"

"You've twisted my arm."

As far as Hermes was concerned Christmas Day was no different to any other. He had no relatives back home, not that he could have contacted anyone if he wanted to, and had not celebrated the event for as long as he could remember. There was no reason to think that today would be any different. Everywhere was closed. It would cause too much suspicion if he turned up at the hospital. From what he had gathered it was highly unusual for a consultant to be there today.

Things had been progressing so well. Gradually over the past few weeks the student nurse had become dependant on her daily "cup of coffee". There had been a noticeable change in the girl, but most people had put this down to the pressure of her upcoming exams. No-one but Hermes knew the real reason. Unfortunately he was now desperately short of heroin. His failure to obtain further supplies had been a major blow. If he had to call a halt now it would mean starting over again. It had been a narrow escape when the drug dealer's flat had been raided. No matter how risky it was he could see no other way to obtain supplies. He would have to try and come up with an alternative. He picked up a biography of Adolf Hitler and settled down for a read.

Pip sat back and put his feet up. He was actually enjoying working on Christmas day. It was now 4 o'clock and in an hours time there would be a Christmas dinner in the medical wards. There was only a handful of patients left in his unit, as all those who were fit enough had been sent home to spend the holiday with their families.

The morning had been taken up in the paediatric ward. Not working though - playing Santa Claus. It had been great fun and made Pip realise that there were some things about the hospital he would miss. Only another two weeks to go and he was off, hopefully to a fresh start, up north.


His mother's Christmas meal has been excellent, as usual. Now, having helped with the clearing up, Angus sat back and relaxed. His sister and brother-in-law, together with their three children, were also at the house. The children were in their element, playing outside in the snow. No doubt when they became fed up with that they would come in and annoy the grown-ups. Still he wouldn't complain. It would give him the opportunity to play with the Scalectrix that he had given Adam as a present.

"I'll just start setting this up here, shall I", said Angus to no-one in particular as he opened the lid on the box.

"I might have known that you would want to play with that"

It was the voice of his mother, who had just come back into the lounge carrying a steaming pot of coffee and a plate of hot mincemeat pies

"Just don't be persuading Adam to take up motor racing. Look what happened to you."

Angus remembered only too well. It had been a bright sunny day when suddenly the heavens opened. Unfortunately for Angus the engine of the car in front had blown up at the same time spewing oil onto the wet track. He, like the other competitors, was still on slick tyres and there was no way he could control the car as he hit the patch of oil and water. The single seater spun wildly and hit a concrete block head-on. A suspension strut had pierced the car and Angus's leg. It had taken the emergency services over an hour to extricate him from the car and it had taken him a further six months to recover. He still had a steel pin in his leg as a legacy of the day.

"I'll let him make his own mind up. It's funny that you should mention it because I was thinking of taking racing up again."

"What! No dear don't do that."

"It's all right. I'll be careful. And anyway it won't be as competitive as before. I just feel that the edge had gone off my driving and that a few laps of the track might be all that I need."

"Be careful. Leave that just now and have your coffee."

**Chapter 16**

The problem with January was Christmas. Once the holiday season was over and the sales had started people had no money. He was in the same position. That was why he had used up a week of his holiday entitlement to do a locum. It was now Wednesday and he was bored - customers had been few and far between. Those that did come into the shop seemed to have an average age of about 85. It was enough to drive any sane person mad - the time wasted listening to them rambling on. 'Coffin dodgers' was how he thought of them, just passing the time until the inevitable happened. Most of them would be better off dead.

The old lady in the shop just now was a perfect example. Mrs French was 89 and on ten different medications. Most of her day must be taken up swallowing pills. As he counted out one of the drugs a thought struck him. He had done it before, capsules could be opened and the contents replaced. If he did it to only one capsule out of the entire bottle then it would never be traced - the evidence would be gone. Today was out of the question though. He would have to get some chemicals out of one of the labs when he returned to work on Monday.

It was a newspaper article about a student demonstration that gave Hermes the idea. Back home the local university had a pharmacology department which held a stock of drugs. It had not been too difficult to find out that there was a polytechnic on the other side of town with a similar department. Security during the day had been virtually non-existent when he had wandered around the sprawling campus. He had discovered that it was tightened slightly after six o'clock when anyone remaining in the building had to inform the security of their presence and the occasional tour round the building by the staff.

It was now eight o'clock and Hermes was waiting in the pharmacology lab. There had been no difficulty remaining in the department without being noticed. Ten minutes previously one of the security had passed on his rounds, checking the door as he passed. Based on the past two hours that he had been waiting in the room Hermes knew that he had about forty minutes before the guard came round again. His investigations had shown him that only three cupboards were locked so presumably the drugs were in one of them.

Hermes removed a set of skeleton keys from his pocket and tried the first cupboard. It opened easily but contained nothing of interest to him - only some exam papers. The second cupboard was equally disappointing - it held only some expensive looking instruments. It had to be the last cupboard. The lock turned easily. At the back was a small safe. It was old and the lock yielded easily. The first thing that he saw was a large black block of raw opium. Hermes ignored it for the time being - the drug was in too crude a state for his use. Then he saw it. An almost full 25 gram jar of diamorphine at the back of the safe. Hermes removed it and placed it on a bench. He removed a small sachet of white powder from his pocket. Opening the jar he tipped half the contents into a small polythene bag which he then sealed. He then transferred the white powder from the sachet into the jar and mixed the contents. To the naked eye there was no way to tell that the jar now contained two powders instead of one. Unless he was unlucky the switch would not be noticed for some time. Now all he had to do was get out of the building unnoticed.

Ten minutes later Hermes was walking back to his car, his future drug supplies safe in his pocket. The half ounce of powder would last him for a month or two because unlike the drugs he had been forced to use this was 100 per cent pure. He would have to be careful with his dosage.

The two men walking to the car rental desk at Heathrow had now been travelling for three weeks. Two days ago they had been in Algiers, totally disheartened. The trail of the man that they were pursuing had gone cold. He had been extremely clever in covering his tracks. It was only a chance encounter in a back street that had led them to Madrid, and from there to England. The man they were after was Claudio Oscar. He had been a high ranking official in their country's previous, military, administration who had abused his power for his own evil ends. They hoped to bring him back for trial to his own country but did not realistically believe that they could accomplish the task and were therefore armed with heavy calibre hand guns. These were dismantled and stowed throughout their luggage in such a way that even the most sophisticated airport security systems could not detect the weapons. The taller of the two dumped their heavy suitcases into the boot as his companion fired up the hired Ford Mondeo. An hour later they were ensconced in adjoining rooms at a nearby hotel.

Immediately on entering the room the smaller of the two, who was known as Guillermo, opened both cases and rapidly emptied them of their contents. Five minutes later the component parts of two heavy automatic handguns, together with 100 rounds of ammunition lay spread out on the dressing table.

"You see Carlo, I told you this new screening material was great stuff. They searched your case completely and found nothing."

"Yes" replied Carlo as he re-assembled his weapon "Just as well for us. Do you think that we'll catch up with our friend Claudio this time?"

"I hope so. All this travelling is doing me no good at all. My body doesn't know what day it is, let alone what time."

"I know how you feel. Tomorrow I think we should just drive up to confirm that our friend is where he should be. If he is as settled as we've been led to believe another day or two of a delay won't matter much. I'd rather rest and plan it carefully. Remember we have to get back out of the country when we've finished."

"Yes." Carlo ran through the action on his gun to check everything was in order. When he was satisfied he put a new clip in the magazine, loaded the first round in the chamber and put on the safety. Guillermo has also finished assembling his gun and he too put a new clip in the magazine, put on the safety and put his gun back at the bottom of the case.


"Timothy, go through and see if your mother's all right. She's been in there a long time."

Timothy ran into the kitchen and re-appeared moments later "Daddy, Daddy. Mummy's lying on the floor.

George Steel dashed into the kitchen to find his wife lying, unconscious, on the floor. After trying unsuccessfully to rouse her he picked up the phone and dialled 999. Ten minutes later the ambulance arrived. Two ambulance men clasped an oxygen mask to the woman's face and transferred her to a stretcher. "Mum, will you look after Timothy while I go to the hospital. You know where everything is. I'll call you as soon as I know anything."

Five minutes later the ambulance arrived at the hospital casualty entrance. The woman was wheeled in, closely followed by her husband. Neil Parsons took one look at the woman and knew that it was virtually hopeless. "What happened here?" he asked as he started to work on her.

"I don't know. She said that she wasn't feeling well and went for a glass of water. When she hadn't appeared ten minutes later I sent my son in to find out what she was doing. He found her lying on the floor.

"She hadn't been taking anything out of the ordinary?"

"No. Well.."

"Yes?"

"She took one of my mothers painkillers."

"Do you have them with you?"

"No."

"Can you find out what they were - maybe phone your mother?"

"Yes. Okay."

"Right. You do that and let us know. It all helps."

Five minutes later Neil gave up. There was no way he was going to be able to revive her. "I'll speak to the husband. Is he waiting outside?"

This was the part of the job that he hated, but it had to be done. Worse was the fact that he had to still get some information form the grieving husband

"It's very important that we have the tablets that she took."

"But my mother's been taking them for three days with no effect."

"All the same, if we could just have a look at them. Had anything else unusual happened?"

"No, she had been fine and she ate the same as the rest of us."

"I'm very sorry. Sister will look after you. If there's anything that we can do.

"Yes. Thank you."

"Dr Hermes. Would you like a cup of coffee?"

"What? Oh yes, thank you."

Becky plugged the kettle in and put coffee into the cups. She couldn't understand what had happened over the past few days. From being friendly towards her the consultant's attitude had changed dramatically - in fact

Dispense With Death

yesterday he had cut her dead. The ward sister had told her to put it down to his Latin temperament.

"Thank you, leave it there" he said, without even looking up as Becky brought over the coffee. It was obvious that he didn't want to talk. Becky left him to it and joined one of the other nurses.

"You know what these Spanish are like, they can be so rude. Just ignore him."

"I suppose so. It's just that he seemed so friendly."

"People are like that - they change from day to day. Speaking of which you've been more like your old self this week."

"What do you mean?"

"Well you seemed a bit down, but you seem to be back to normal - were the exams getting to you?"

"No. I didn't seem to be able to concentrate for them but I think that I did all right. And then I took the flu after Christmas, at least I think that's what it was - I was shivering all over, runny nose, sweats the lot."

"Oh well then. Lets hope the results are good when they come out tomorrow".


Angus pulled on his helmet and squeezed himself into the single seater Formula Ford 1600. Although it was bitterly cold the combination of fireproof undergarments, his overalls and the helmet meant that he could feel the sweat trickling down his arms - and he hadn't started driving yet.

A mechanic fired up the engine and the noise of the virtually unsilenced engine behind his right ear pounded into his brain. Gently Angus put the car into gear and drove to the start line. The last time he had sat in a car like this a friend used a stop watch to time the laps. Now it was all hi-tech. The car had an infra- red transmitter built into the nose cone. When he started a lap it broke a beam and started the clock. Then when he crossed the finish line it broke another beam and his lap time flashed up instantaneously on a screen at the right hand side of the track. The light changed to green and he was off. A short burst up the straight and it was hard on the brakes for a 90o left hander followed immediately by a 90o right. Oops. Got that wrong. The offside rear wheel hit the rumble strip and kicked the back end off line. Angus corrected and caught it before he spun. Now it was another short straight before a sweeping left hander that tightened just when you didn't expect it.

Angus buried his right foot to the floor as he exited the curve. All too soon he had to ease for a gentle left turn followed by a tight hairpin. Now the circuit began to climb and he piled on the power again. A sharp dip left and his stomach was somewhere in his helmet as the track plunged down to a complex series of bends - right, tight hairpin followed by a 90o left hander. Now he was on the longest straight on the circuit and he could really feel the wind on his face. Then he realised why. the gloved left hand came off the steering wheel and pulled down the visor. The straight ended with a sweeping curve to the left which scrubbed off some speed without the need to use the brakes. Then it was into the braking zone before another hairpin. Another series of curves completed the lap. Angus looked up to see his time - 85 seconds. Not that good. Still it was his first lap for how many years?

He set off again. By the time he was halfway through the lap he knew that he was faster. The time on the display backed him up - 72 seconds. By the end of ten laps his time had come down to 67 seconds. Now he was only managing to take the odd half second a lap off the time, but it was an improvement. The next lap was a disaster. He got the line all wrong for the complex of bends and the car spun to a halt on the hairpin exit. The grass and dirt that the tyres picked up destroyed his grip and he slowly brought the car back to the pits.

"You were going well until then." The mechanic turned off the ignition.

"I was too confident. There'll be more of those no doubt before I'm finished. I'm going for some lunch - how about you?"

"Right. Give us a hand to wheel this back in, will you?"

## Chapter 17

John Blackwell was bored. The Sales Department of Neuroscience Pharmaceuticals was working flat out to fill the rush of orders following the Christmas and New Year shutdown but up here in the Quality Control laboratory things were deadly quiet. The production unit had just restarted this morning and it would take a day or two for work to filter through to him. He pulled down the file containing last year's customer complaints and flicked through it. Considering the range of products that the company produced the file was surprisingly thin - only about 100 pages.

When he came to record of the atropine complaint he stopped. He remembered all the panic it had caused at the time - his boss had been called in late on a Saturday night to deal with the case. Reading through the file it all came flooding back. He had had to work on the Sunday analysing the samples - and found nothing amiss. He quickly scanned through the tests he had carried out - the full final product specification - and it had passed them all.

Wait a minute though. He had tested the sample on the basis that there was something wrong with the active ingredient, not looking for something else. When he had found the atropine content to be correct he had been satisfied. But what if something else had been added to the vials. If it didn't interfere with the atropine assay he would not necessarily have spotted it.

He removed the set of keys from his desk drawer and walked down the corridor to the samples store. Each report was given a number so if there was any sample left he should be able to find it quickly. Had he used it

Dispense With Death

all up - he couldn't really remember. There it was. On the top shelf - sample 90/081. two vials still left. he removed them and made a note on the accompanying bin card. When he returned to the lab he placed the samples on the desk and pulled out a thick reference book from the bookcase. Now. What else could there have been in the vials? Fifteen minutes later he put the book down, switched on his instruments and set to work.

He re-checked the results again, just to make sure. There it was again. Definitely a high concentration of pralidoxime in the sample. He had noticed reports of the two agents antagonising each other although it had not been proved conclusively. If he was correct, and he was sure that he was, there could be far reaching consequences from this. Someone must have added the pralidoxime to the vial. Surely it couldn't have been someone in the factory. The controls during manufacture were too strict. Weren't they? It should be relatively easy to tell whether the vial had been tampered with. His department had recently invested in a new scanning electron microscope. If he was lucky he might be able to determine how often the rubber bung in the vial had been punctured. He laid the paperwork aside and walked down the corridor to the production department.

"Morning Jim. Can I take a bag of these bungs?"

"Sure. Just fill this form in first though, will you."

John filled in the form and walked back to his office. That was why he was so sure that any adulteration couldn't have taken place in the factory. Every step was logged. The form he had just filled in would form part of a record somewhere. Having said that if someone was determined..

\*\*\*

Morning Ben. Did you have a good week off?"

"Not bad. I ended up doing a locum - you know - to replace the cash spent at Christmas."

"Me too. Still it makes a change from working in here."

"Too true. Listen what are you doing at lunchtime - fancy going down the road for a pub lunch?"

"Excellent idea. Being stuck in a shop for a week over lunchtimes I've had my fill of sandwiches. Half twelve all right with you?"

"Fine. I've got to help out Miss McLean this week so I'd better go. See you later."

\*\*\*

It took an hour to prepare the samples. First of all he examined ten bungs chosen at random from the bag he had taken from the store. Under the high magnification every imperfection on the rubber surface showed up on the screen. With the exception a few variations each was the same. Then he placed the bung from the hospital sample in the instrument.

At the extreme magnification each needle puncture looked like a massive peak standing proud of the flat landscape. It was unmistakable - three jagged tears in the rubber. therefore it followed that three needles had punctured the bung. One of those he had made himself only yesterday, and another when he had originally assayed the sample. That left one unaccounted for. He quickly checked the paperwork in the file. There was the original letter from the hospital

"Please find enclosed our remaining stock of this batch from the Pharmacy. Unfortunately the vials used in the incident have been destroyed."

That seemed to point to the sample having been a new vial. It followed then that the vial had been tampered with. He picked up the phone, then hesitated. Having made up his mind he dialled an internal number. Five minutes later he hung up, dialled the hospital number and was put through to the Pharmacy.

"Miss Smith? Neuroscience Pharmaceuticals here. You sent some samples to us for analysis some months back. Atropine injection. Do you remember?"

"Yes." How could she forget.

"We're just tidying up some paperwork here. Can you confirm whether the samples you sent were unused vials, or ones that had been used by Doctor Barton."

"Definitely untouched. I took them off our shelves myself."

"That's fine. Thanks for your help."

Just then one of the pharmacy staff came into the office

"What's up? You look confused."

Helene replaced the phone on the cradle. "So would you be. Remember that incident a couple of months ago - with Doctor Barton?"

"Uh huh"

"That's Neuroscience on the phone about it. I thought that it was all over and done with."

"So did I. What did they want?"

"Just to confirm whether the vials were the ones used by Doctor Barton or stock from our shelves. Strange."

"Yes" said Helene's colleague as he returned to what he was doing.

"We have two choices. Either someone in the factory contaminated the vials, or someone in the distribution chain. Where else had these vials been?"

Once he had come off the phone John Blackwell had contacted his boss, Andrina Burnside, who had called the meeting now taking place. Also present were Irvine Ogg, the distribution director and William Balfe, the firm's medical director.

"Just the factory and the hospital" It was Irvine Ogg who spoke up. "Unless, of course they bought some from a local wholesaler. I think that's unlikely though. They buy the product from us fairly regularly so I would concentrate on the factory first of all."

"Fair enough. Bill - what's the likelihood that the combination that John found could have caused the patient's death?"

"I wouldn't like to say for certain. As John points out there have been reports of the two drugs antagonising each other. Equally there are reports of them being used together. Without more information on the two patients concerned we can't say for certain. I don't think, though, that we should try to get that information unless it is really necessary. And by that I mean until we are sure that the contamination didn't happen in this building."

"Agreed. Irvine, can you backtrack through the records and find out who was on duty the day that batch was made. Who had the opportunity to contaminate it. Anyone who may have had a grudge against the company. that sort of thing. Remember there may have been more than one vial tampered with so the person involved could have needed a reasonable amount of time unobserved.
Bill, can you find any information that you can on mixtures of these two products.
John, can you check back the lab records for the batch - look for the same things that I've outlined to Irvine. That's all gentlemen. We'll meet back here tomorrow at 9 o'clock". With that Andrina closed her file, stood up, and walked out the room.

\* \* \*

"Gentlemen, I'm sure that some of you already know Louis Forbes from our legal department. He'll listen in on today's meeting and give us his advice. Now what do we have?"

William Balfe handed round copies of a report he had prepared on atropine and pralidoxime. "As you can see there isn't too much information. But if the patient was compromised an interaction between the drugs could have been enough to tip them over the edge."

"Irvine?"

"Nothing. Absolutely no way that I can see contamination taking place on the production line or in the warehouse. Most of the people on the line are locals who wouldn't want to harm the firm. If we folded this whole town would go with us. Besides none of them would have access to the compounds involved here."

"A relative or friend could."

"True, but I still think unlikely."

"John?"

"I don't see it coming from the lab end either - for two reasons. First we have never had cause to use pralidoxime and two, we only receive a few samples of the batch for testing and storage purposes. If someone removed vials from the batch it would have been noticed."

"What about the raw material for the batch itself. Could it have been contaminated?"

"It could gave been. However the powder dissolves easily and would have been well mixed during production. I can see no way that the high concentration of pralidoxime that I found could have been in only one small part of the batch."

"So as far as you are all concerned we appear to be in the clear?" Nods from around the table.

"Louis, what do you see our legal position as being?"

"It is impossible for the company to state categorically that it is not responsible for this contamination. From what Andrina has already told me and the information in front of me today I would say that it is reasonable to state that we are not responsible. That basically means that the hospital we supplied the product to, or more accurately someone working at the hospital, is responsible. The only way to prove that is to involve the police. I submit that our next course of action should be to document all that we have done so far and inform the hospital."

"What if we send the information to the person that was responsible - they might just ignore it or try to cover it up?"

"I'll send a copy to the hospital general manager as well." Andrina had already foreseen that possibility. "That way there's bound to be some action. Can you put it all together this afternoon?"

"Yes."

"When you have done that I'll have a covering letter typed up and send off copies to the hospital. I'll phone them too. I suppose it's only fair to give them advance warning."

\* \* \*

"Shit!"

"Something wrong?"

"That was the head of Quality Control at Neuroscience Pharmaceuticals. Do you remember that case a while back involving Doctor Barton, when he thought that there was something wrong with the drugs on the cardiac arrest trays?"
Ben remembered the incident and said so "I thought there was nothing in it."

"So did I at the time but now it seems not. They were re-examining the vials that we sent and found something wrong. I don't know what yet, the chap didn't say on the phone. They're sending all the documentation up by post, including a copy to the General Manager. I can see all hell breaking loose."

"Doctor Parsons, we've got the result of the post mortem on Mrs Steel."
Neil put down the notes he had been reading and picked up the report. "Are you sure that this is correct?"

"I can phone and check if you like"

"Would you do that?"

Five minutes later the ward sister returned. "No doubt. A massive heart attack, caused most likely by acute digoxin poisoning."

"Her husband told me it was a painkiller that she took. Let's see. Yes, here we are - mefenamic acid which had been prescribed for her mother. He came back in with the bottle yesterday. I think I should go and have a word with him."

Hermes tipped the diamorphine into a small bowl. From one of his cases he removed two small vials of white powder. One was stramonium, a potent

Dispense With Death

hallucinogen. The action of the other he was not totally sure of - yet. The contents of these two vials joined the diamorphine in the bowl. Then, using a kitchen knife, he carefully mixed the three powders for five minutes. When he had finished he laid a sheet of kitchen foil on the table and cut it into 2" squares. After laying these out he placed a small quantity of powder into the middle of each one, gradually increasing the quantity on each successive square until the bowl was empty.

This task completed he carefully folded each square to enclose the powder. He had just finished folding the last one when the doorbell rang. As he turned to stand up his arm brushed over the table and knocked three of the packets to the floor. Hermes bent down and put them back on the table. Two minutes later he returned to his task having sent the double glazing salesman away with a flea in his ear. Anyone walking into the block with their eyes open could see that that every flat already had double glazing fitted. As he turned back to the table he noticed that three of the packets did not seem to be laid out the same as the others. He tidied them into position and set about numbering the packets.

Neil parked the car and walked across the quiet street. This was one of the better areas of town. Populated by middle manager types, as evidenced by the rows of BMW's and Volvo's parked along the street, it had not suffered too badly when the car plant had closed down. He pushed open the gate and walked up the neat gravel path. There were no children in the garden. This was a house still in mourning. He rang the door bell.

"Dr Parsons. What are you doing here?" It was George Steel. "Sorry, come on in."

"I hope that I'm not intruding. I just want to ask you a few questions."

"Yes" Tears welled up in the man's eyes as he turned away, hand in pocket reaching for his handkerchief. "Come in here. The children are at their other grandparents. It's the funeral tomorrow so I wanted to get things organised with them out of the way. I don't think they realise quite what's happened yet. Come to think of it I don't think I do either."

"These things take time. Your mother, is she on any other medication, except for the painkillers?"

"Yes. She takes tablets for her heart and for her breathing."

"Can I see them?"

"Of course. Is there anything wrong?"

"No I just want to check a few things that I didn't have time to at the hospital."
Neil watched as the man left the room. He was wrecked. Although he didn't seem to know it yet it was obvious to an outsider that his wife's sudden death had hit him - hard. George Steel returned holding four bottle of tablets.

"Here you are."

Neil read the labels and checked the contents in each bottle. The first was the mefenamic acid, which he laid to one side. The second was the unfinished remainder of a course of antibiotics from six months back. When would people take these drugs seriously? The third bottle contained the woman's salbutamol tablets and the

Dispense With Death

last would surely be digoxin. But no, they were not. Bang went that theory.

"There's no others ? Old bottles that she no longer takes ?"

"No. she's been on the same tablets for years. Just gets a repeat each month."

"Nobody else in the house on any medication ? Yourself? Any visitors?"

"No. Why?"

"Your wife wasn't taking any medication for her heart?"

"No. What is it? What's going on?"

"Your wife died of a heart attack. We found a drug in her body that's normally taken by someone with a heart complaint."

"You think she took some of my mother's other tablets by mistake?"

"Yes, but it wasn't any of these three here. You're sure that it was these that she took" pointing to the mefenamic acid.

"Positive. They were on the worktop when I when I" George Steel burst into tears. "I'm sorry."

"Don't be daft. There's no shame in crying. It's much worse to bottle grief up inside. If there's anything I can do."

"No, it's okay. I'll be fine"

"Can I take these" indicating the painkillers. "I can leave a prescription for more if you like."

"Take them. Just get them out of here."

Neil pocketed the bottle, made his goodbyes and drove back to the hospital. He looked at the chemist's name on the bottle. It was fairly local, but one that Neil had never been in. He knew some people up at the hospital pharmacy so decided to phone there instead.

"It's Dr Parsons here. I have some capsules that I would like analysed. can you do it?"

"Do you know what they are?"

"Mefenamic acid. But I think that there is something wrong with them."

"What do you mean?"

"A patient died after taking them."

"Did they come from this hospital?" Helene had a terrible feeling of deja vu.

"No they were dispensed by a local chemist"

A sigh of relief

"And have you contacted them?"

"No. I thought of you first. Can you help?"

"Send them up and we'll have a look at them."

Dispense With Death

"Thanks."

Helene looked at the bottle. The contents certainly looked, to her, like mefenamic acid but as the capsules were unmarked it could have been one of dozens of companies who had made them. She knew that the Department of Health ran a drug testing scheme to test the accuracy of prescriptions but from what she had heard about the system it could take weeks to get a result back. Doctor Parsons had sounded as if he wanted the result yesterday - not next month. And as for his last comment - "Look for digoxin" - what was that supposed to mean?. The hospital had a biochemistry department that carried out routine digoxin assays on patients. Helene decided to send them a sample. After counting out five of the capsules into a bottle she filled out a form and had the pharmacy porter take the sample along to Biochemistry. That result should be back by tomorrow. The remainder of the bottle she parcelled up and sent to the Department of Health. When she would hear from them was anyone's guess.

## Chapter 18

Donald Layne was furious. A scandal like this would ruin his future career prospects in the Health Service. As soon as he had received the letter he had contacted Val McLean demanding to know what was going on.

Due to the way the internal mail system worked Val had not yet received her letter from Neuroscience and so was one step behind her General Manager. She had been summonsed to his office along with anyone else involved in the incident. Sitting along with her in the office were Helene and Miss Sven, Doctor Barton being unavailable having left the hospital, waiting for Layne's next outburst.

"Can I see the letter?"

Layne threw the piece of paper across the desk at her.

"I haven't received a copy of this yet" said Val as she scanned the letter's contents. "All I've had is a phone call from the company" an admission she regretted immediately.

"And what did you do about it" jumping down her throat.

"Nothing."

"What do you mean nothing. This hospital is accused of killing people and you sit back and do nothing."

Dispense With Death

"Of course not" Val was getting in deeper and deeper. "All they said on the phone was that they had re-examined the vials and were sending a copy of the results."

"And you didn't think of asking for any further information?"

"No"

"Brilliant. Well now that we all know what the problem is we have to sort it out. Any ideas how it could have taken place?"

"It could have on the ward or in the pharmacy" Helene spoke for the first time.

"The trays are sealed when we receive them on the ward and any that show any sign of being opened are sent back to pharmacy." said Miss Sven, anxious to divert any blame away from her staff.

"Is this true? Could a tray get to a ward, be tampered with and not be noticed?"

"It's unlikely. The seals that we use are not very strong. After all people don't have time to waste when they're using the tray. It is a life and"

"Yes. Yes. So we should be looking at the pharmacy and its staff. You had the police in recently didn't you. One of your staff switched some tablets and almost killed a patient."

"I wouldn't say almost killed a patient!"

"Well I would. It was lucky she didn't hit her head or something when she fell. Anyway what are you going to do about this. Could it be connected."

"We've already gone over this ground."

"Well go over it again. I want to see you all here tomorrow morning at 8am sharp, with the proper answers."

Layne pressed a button on his intercom.

"Miss Davis. Could you find out which hospital a Doctor Barton, who used to work here, is working at now." He looked at Miss Sven "When did he leave here?"

"Just after Christmas"

"Did you get that. Good. When you find out can you get him on the phone for me. Thanks."

"You can go. And remember, eight o'clock tomorrow."

Helene hadn't believed the result when she had first seen it and had phoned biochemistry to confirm. It appeared that one of the five capsules she had sent contained enough digoxin to kill a horse.

"Paul, you've worked as a locum at this shop, haven't you?"

Paul Rannachan looked at the label.

"Yes, I was there last week. Why?"

Helene recounted the tale as she knew it.

"You don't think someone did it on purpose, do you?"

"It certainly looks Hello. Doctor Parsons? That sample you sent up yesterday - any reason why you said to look for digoxin?"

"What have you found?"

"I sent a sample to biochem. One of the capsules contained enough digoxin to kill "

"A woman"

"More than that."

"You're sure of this?"

"Positive."

"Right. I'll be up to see you in five minutes. Is that okay?"

"Yes." Helene hung up.

"Let me see the bottle" Paul took it from Helene's hand. "Thank goodness. It wasn't dispensed last week. For a minute there I thought I was in deep shit."

"Whoever did this, and I doubt very much that it was an accident, is in more than deep shit, as you put it. I think a murder charge could be on the cards"

"Bloody hell."

The bell at the hatch rang. Paul walked out and recognising Neil let him into the department.

Dispense With Death

"We had an apparent accidental death, a young woman, a couple of days ago. When the post mortem showed a high digoxin level I became suspicious, particularly so when there appeared no opportunity for her to have taken the drug."

Helene told him how only one of the capsules contained digoxin, the other four being normal.

"I would bet that the rest of the sample is okay. You know that if whoever did this had only contaminated one capsule we would have no evidence to go on."

"What age was she?"

"27. With two young kids. The real tragedy is that it wasn't even her medicine. The old granny lives with the family and the drugs were prescribed for her."
"So someone wanted to put the old dear out of her misery?" said Paul.

"That doesn't make it any better " said Helene.

"No. I didn't mean it like that."

"What do we do now" said Neil "call the police?"

"I think we should let Miss McLean know first and let her make the decision. She's going to love this."

It was now 5 o'clock and Val thought it pointless to keep the staff behind. It wasn't really a hospital matter anyway - they had only become involved by default. After discussions with Dr Parsons she decided to wait until morning to call the police.

Guillermo unpacked the cases within five minutes of entering the room. He had long since mastered the knack - moving quickly was often a matter of life and death in his profession. Carlo had dropped him at the hotel entrance and driven on to check that their quarry was still where they wanted him. He turned quickly as the door opened.

"Be more careful. You could get yourself killed sneaking up like that."

"Relax" said Carlo "you always get like this before a hit. He suspects nothing. In fact he is still keeping to the routine we were told of. I think we should make a move tomorrow night."

Well,well,well. It looked as if he had been right all along. Pip had been surprised when the hospital General Manager had called him. It was now 10 o'clock and he had just come off duty. He was faced with a drive through the night in order to make the meeting for 8 o'clock tomorrow morning. Still, he could put up with that if it finally meant that he could clear his name. He pulled on a jacket and walked out to his car.

**Chapter 19**

He was confused. The salesman had assured him that this was one of the fastest cars on the market yet his pursuers seemed to be gaining. He was doing over one hundred miles an hour. The girl beside him was clinging onto the door handle trying to stay in her seat.

A face suddenly pulled level with his window. It was an old woman, at least 90. He looked closer. She was in a wheelchair! Looking in his mirror he could see dozens more of them and behind them at least three police cars.

There was a strange burring noise at the driver's door. The old woman was trying to drill her way into the car. He pulled the wheel violently to the left to escape her. Too late he saw the cliff edge. His girlfriend screamed and the car hit the rocks.

He looked up. He was lying on the bedroom floor, his bedside alarm buzzing to waken him.

Eight o'clock in the morning. Pip parked his car and walked into the hospital administration block. He was absolutely shattered. Twice on the drive through he had had to stop at a service station and go walkabout when he felt himself nodding off at the wheel. He knocked on the General Manager's door and walked in.

"Doctor Parsons. Glad that you could join us at such short notice. Do sit down.
I'm Donald Layne. I think you know everyone else here."

"Yes, thank you."

"This is a copy of what we have so far" said Layne, handing over a copy of the previous day's report. "I'll give you a few minutes to read through before we start."

Pip quickly scanned the first page, which told him nothing new, and flipped over to the second page.

"Bloody hell! Sorry."

There was a knock at the door and Val McLean walked into the room.

"You're late."

"Yes. I'm sorry but I had to call the police before I came here."

"What do you mean. It was decided to wait until after this meeting before taking any action."

"I know" replied Val and proceeded to recount the events of the previous afternoon.

"Do you think that the two events could be connected?" Pip had finished the report and looked at Val.

"I don't know. It is really unusual for something like this to happen. For two occurrences in the same area in such a short space of time would be some coincidence."

"How could there be a connection between the hospital and this shop you mentioned?" Layne asked.

"A number of the staff do locums at the shop. Saturdays, the odd week here and there."

"I see. Do you know exactly which members of your staff?"

Val handed over a slip of paper containing four names

"Fine. Has anyone else managed to get any further with this?"

A series of Noes from around the table.

"Can I suggest something?" asked Pip

"Go ahead."

"I presume that you are going to involve the police in this" indicating the paper in front of him. Layne nodded. "Well, if we assume. and it seems not unreasonable to do so, that the same person was responsible for both these acts I think that we should inform the police of our suspicions. The four names on that list you have must be prime candidates."

"Much as I hate to admit it I have to agree with you" said Val.

"Are these four at work today?"

"Yes."

"What time are the police due?"

"9 o'clock."

Dispense With Death

"Right I will come back to pharmacy with you. We'll do as Dr Barton suggests. How many other people know about this?"

"Just the five of us" replied Val.

"Right, it goes no further for the moment.

"Well actually." Helene spoke up for the first time.

"Yes" Layne guessed what was to come.

"I think that some others know about this. Ben Brosan was there when the company phoned, and Paul Rannachan knows about the shop incident."

"Brilliant. And those are two of the names on this list. There's one other thing. A month or so back a reporter from the local paper came to me with some cock and bull story, claiming that there had been a series of suspicious deaths in the hospital. It was dismissed at the time as scandal mongering. Now I'm not so sure. I think that we should let the police know and see if they want to take it further."

"You mean that this nutter has killed even more people" shouted Pip "and for all these months I've been carrying the blame for one of the deaths."

"Nobody blamed you, and I think we should all stay calm about this, there's no point in becoming hysterical. Right it's ten to nine, time we headed over to the pharmacy. Thank you once again for taking the trouble to come through at such short notice Dr Parsons. You can rest assured that I personally will put a note in your file about your part in this matter. It's just a pity that your suspicions weren't proved correct sooner - who knows it may have saved that young woman's life. Still there's no blame attached to anyone here that I can see. We just struck lucky that some lab technician was bored after the holidays.

Hermes came in early. In his pocket was the weakest dose from the foil sachets that he had prepared. Becky was just about to have her break.

"I'll make the coffee, you sit down."

"Thank you " said Becky, surprised by his attitude, "it's been a busy morning so far."

Hermes tipped the contents of the sachet into the mug. He poured in the coffee and stirred until the effervescence had died down.

"Drink this, you'll soon feel better."

"Thanks."

It took five minutes before the drugs started to take effect.

"The dragons are flying in through the window. Look out!".

"What?" Hermes looked up.

"They're heading over here. Get away." Becky screamed and lashed out with her arm. The remains of her mug of coffee crashed to the floor, spilling some of the hot liquid on her hand.

"Aargh. The dragon's burnt my wrist."

"Nurse Donaldson, control yourself!" The ward sister had come over because of the commotion.

"He's at my throat. Stop it. Get away. I can't breathe."

Becky collapsed on the floor. Hermes rushed over to her. She had stopped breathing. Too much diamorphine. But how? The packets. When he was preparing them he had knocked some over. He must have mixed them up when he picked them up.

"Sister. Get the cardiac arrest tray quick, and some diamorphine.
Hermes went through the motions, as though it were a real arrest. By the time the crash team arrived it was too late - Becky was dead.

"Poor girl. She was only 19. She was due to be married soon. Her fiancé! He works in the hospital, who's going to tell him?"

"I think that we should tell her parents first" said Hermes. "Do you know where she stays sister?"

"Her father's a porter in the hospital. I'll get him to the ward on some pretext."

Angus and Norman were back in Val McLean's office. They had interviewed the first two names on the list.

"Can you send Paul Rannachan in please?"

Paul was walking towards the office. As he passed the hatch he noticed a porter standing, looking extremely distraught.

"Can I help you?"

Dispense With Death

"Is Ben in?"

"Hold on and I'll get him."

A few moments later Ben appeared at the hatch. "What's wrong Tom?"

"I think that you should sit down.

"Why?" Ben did as he was asked.

"I don't know how to tell you this."

""What is it ? Becky?"

"Yes. She's dead.

"What!"

"A short time ago. In the ward. It seems that she had a heart attack. They did what they could but it was no use. It was all over very quickly."

"But I spoke to her this morning. She was all right then. Are you sure?"

"Yes. I know. I'm as confused as you are. She's never had any trouble like this before. They did their best on the ward, apparently, but it was no use. I'm going home just now. Do you want to come back with me?"

"No. I'll be all right. I'll go back to the flat. I'd rather be on my own."

**Chapter 20**

Angus pulled up outside the shop. The interviews at the hospital had been inconclusive. He should have started out at the shop and found out who had been on duty the day that the drugs were dispensed.

The pharmacist, Elizabeth Dine, had already had a visit from the local police earlier that morning and so was not surprised when Angus came into the shop.
"I showed your colleague the locum book."

"Can I see it anyway while I'm here please. I think our paths have crossed with the local lads. I didn't realise that they had already been in."

Mrs Dine retrieved the book from her office drawer and turned to the relevant page.

"There you are. February 8th. Paul Rannachan was working here that day."
"We've already spoken to him. I see that you had a locum in for the rest of the week?"

"I was up at the Lake District for a holiday. Always go there this time of year. Ben always does that week for me. I don't know why he didn't do the Saturday though, he usually does the whole week. I thought that this year of all years he would have needed the money."

"Yes. I see. Now just a couple more details. Where did you obtain your stock of the drug?"

"We buy those direct from the manufacturer, Neuroscience. I've got their address somewhere."

Mrs Dine pulled a bottle of tablets from the shelf and pointed out the address to Angus, who copied it into his notebook. "Thank you."

"What happens now?"

"We'll get in touch with this company first of all and see if they can shed any light on things. I would suggest that you contact your insurers, if you haven't already done so."

"I 'phoned them this morning."

"Good. Better to let them know as soon as possible. We'll going now."

Angus pulled the Lotus out into the traffic.

"Well what do you think?"

"Back to interview Paul Rannachan again?"

"I think so. He told us that he wasn't working that day but the shop's record shows otherwise. Radio in and have a Panda car go to the hospital and take him down to the station. The shock of that might persuade him to tell the truth this time."

"What do we do now?"

"Pay a visit to Mr Brosan. No, on second thoughts lets meet Mr Rannachan at the station. With any luck we can get this wrapped up today."

Hermes pulled into his parking place. He noticed the Ford parked across the street. The driver was sitting

Dispense With Death

reading a newspaper. From his viewpoint Hermes took him to be of Latin origin. He was immediately on his guard. As he walked into the building he glanced behind him. The man was still in the car.

Hermes turned the key in the lock and opened the door to his flat. The next he knew he was lying sprawled in the middle of the lounge floor. He turned round to find himself staring up at the silencer on the end of an automatic pistol, behind which he recognised the face of his old subordinate Guillermo Mendoza.

"So Claudio, we have caught up with you at last. You didn't really think that you could get away with it did you?"

Hermes made to get up but was stopped by a well placed kick in the stomach.

"Stay where you are. Don't try anything. Remember I know you. I know how you think."

"You deceitful bastard. All those years you worked with me. How much did they pay you. Whatever it is I'll double it."

"Don't waste your breath. I don't need your money. I'm doing this because I want to. All those years I worked with you. Suffered working under you more like. I was glad to see the end of your tyrannical little regime. You just made it out the country by the skin of your teeth. We just missed you by about 10 minutes. You've led us a merry dance."

"Who is we?"

"You'll find out soon enough."

"What are you going to do with me? Take me back?" Hermes shifted onto one knee. Guillermo smashed the gun across his face, breaking his jaw in the process.

"I told you not to move." Guillermo stepped back. "Why should we take you back. The government would prefer it of course. A nice show trial would do their image the world of good. But if we have to kill you because you resist then no-one will shed a tear. It's a pity really."

"Spare me the crap" Hermes was thinking wildly, trying to find a way out of the situation.

"No, no. It's true. You see things will revert back to the old ways and they'll need someone to fill your old job."

"Which I suppose will be you?"

A sudden noise at the door caused Guillermo to turn around. It was just the opportunity Hermes needed. He dived to his right and reached behind the display unit. He pulled the gun free that he had taped to the back of the unit. Guillermo had turned back, seeing his partner come in through the door. He saw Hermes hand behind the unit, raised his gun and fired. The hammer hit an empty chamber. Before he had time to wonder what had gone wrong Hermes had fired. The first shot caught Guillermo in the chest. As he doubled over Hermes fired again. The top of Guillermo's head disintegrated as the bullet entered, spraying the room with a fine grey mist. As the body fell to the floor Hermes just had time to see his would be assassin's partner in the doorway, his gun aimed straight at him, before everything went black.

Dispense With Death

"Are you trying to tell me that you were not working on that day?"

"Yes. I was going to work it for Ben because he couldn't do it. Then he phoned me during the week and said would I mind if he worked the Saturday after all because he needed the money."

Rannachan was close to tears following having been kept waiting for fifteen minutes of relentless before Angus started his questioning.

"Then why was your name still in the book?"

"I told you. I don't know. Wait. Maybe the manager had organised the locum money before she went on holiday. Ben and I swapped during the week so my name would already have been in the book."

"Then why wasn't the book altered?"

"I never thought to say and presumably Ben didn't either."

"It would have saved a lot of trouble if you had told us this in the first place."

"But I did. How was I to know that the shop records would say that I was working there when I wasn't. Phone the shop. the staff there will confirm it."

"Don't worry. We will" Angus nodded to Norman, who left the interview room. He felt a fool. Why had he not thought of that when he was in the shop.

Five minutes Norman returned and confirmed that Ben had indeed worked on the Saturday in question.

After Rannachan has left Angus sat back down in his office.

"Do we visit Brosan now?" asked Norman.

"I suppose so. You know Norman the longer this goes on the more I'm convinced that there's something that were either missing or know nothing about. You saw what that shop was like. It was pandemonium. How could someone carry out this substitution without it being noticed. There was hardly any room to swing a cat in there. I really think that the answer lies elsewhere. Let's leave Mr Brosan for today. I don't think that he'll be going anywhere for the next few days. Have we made any progress with this drug company yet?"

"This just came in and very interesting it is too. The company thought that we were enquiring about another drug problem involving the hospital."

Norman recounted his conversation with the boss at Neuroscience.

"So our local hospital seems to be having a fair bit of trouble these days. I think that we should pay them another visit tomorrow."

## Chapter 21

Angus knocked on the door of the flat. When there was no reply after a couple of minutes he turned the door handle.

"Mr Brosan. Are you here?"

No reply. Angus opened the bedroom door. Ben was lying motionless on top of the bed.

"Is he asleep?" asked Norman.

"I don't think so. Look at this." Angus picked up an empty tablet bottle from the bedside table.

"Looks like he's taken the lot. Here's the seal from the bottle.

Angus checked for a pulse. There was none.

"Sir, there's a note on the dresser."

"Read it out. What is it? His confession because he knew we were on to him?"

"I don't know " Norman started to read the note ""Why did she have to die. I didn't mean it to happen.""

"I told you so."

"Wait a minute there's more "I loved her. Now I'll be with her forever. Please forgive me." That's about his fiancee. She died this morning. Poor guy. He just couldn't take it. But it doesn't make sense. She died of a heart attack. He didn't kill her. "

Angus was quiet for a moment.

"Didn't he?" said Norman.

Just then his radio burst into life. "Come on Norman. there's been a shooting down the road. We'll leave this to the local lads and finish it off later.

Dispense With Death

**About the author**

Peter Mulholland is a pharmacist working in a Neonatal Intensive Care Unit in the NHS in the UK. He has published several papers in his field and has presented at UK and European conferences. In 2008 he was awarded the College of Pharmacy Practice Balmford Silver Jubilee Award

He is also a keen photographer winning the 2013 Tennis Scotland / MacMillan Cancer Photo competition, and has had photographs published in several magazines.

Dispense With Death is his first novel

www.petermulholland.wordpress.com

Author photograph © Rutherglen Reformer 2013

Printed in Great Britain
by Amazon.co.uk, Ltd.,
Marston Gate.